Love
Granps & Carled x x

Lesley is our friend

Lightning

Lesley Cheetham

To Noah,

love from

Lesley Cheetham

First published in 2014 by LambChop Publishing
and Albury Books
Albury Court, Albury,
Thame, Oxfordshire, OX9 2LP

www.alburybooks.com

A CIP catalogue record for this title is available from the British Library

ISBN 978-0-9572858-3-5

Printed and bound by CPI Group (UK) Ltd, Croydon, CR0 4YY

Lightning

Lesley Cheetham

Lambchop Publishing

Also by Lesley Cheetham

Her Sister's Voice
Her Other Voice
Someone Like Me

To Charlie and Alfie, my favourite lightning sparks.

PROLOGUE

*S*he stepped out from under the tree. No longer protected, icy drops of rain poured down her neck and she started to shake. The second bout of thunder was followed closely by a cracking sound as a white shard of lightning zigzagged down from the sky and struck the ground in front of her, a flash hitting her straight through the eyes. She recoiled as her irises burned and she was knocked from her feet.

Almost instantly, the rain eased off and the air became stiller, quieter. She waited a few moments then opened her eyes. Everything in her sightline dazzled like a polished diamond. She was different now.

CHAPTER 1

Bramble Cottage was out in the wilds. Elise had no idea where the closest neighbour was. The weirdest thing was the silence at night time. Not even the sound of a bird to pierce through the stillness in that annoying way they had, first thing in the morning when she was trying to sleep.

As she walked downstairs that morning, the hallway seemed to take on a different character. Light streamed in through the glass panes in the front door, catching the gilt frame of a painting that hung behind the door. She hadn't noticed it when they'd arrived last night. It was hard to believe it was only a painting, the light on the face too real. It was a portrait of a young girl. She had long dark hair and her eyes were green, almost yellow. Her features were somehow familiar. Something about it made Elise feel cold inside.

Mum was sitting at the large table in the kitchen, sipping a mug of tea. The back door was open and the early morning sun was trickling in, making patterns on the floor. Elise paused for a moment in the doorway. She liked it best when it was like this, just the two of them. She pulled a chair up into the sunlight to catch some rays on her skin, and reached out for the pot to pour herself some tea.

'Did you sleep well?' Mum asked.

'It's so quiet, Mum, so different.'

Elise stirred the tea, her eyes taking in the pile of papers and books set out on the table. 'What's that?' she asked. Two cardboard boxes stood on the floor.

'It's stuff Aunt Celia left in the attic upstairs. There are boxes and boxes of papers up there.'

'Attic? I didn't know there was one.'

'You wouldn't like it at all. There's no light and it smells musty. I wouldn't be surprised if there are small creatures living in the walls.'

'Have you been up there?'

Mum's eyes took on a faraway look. 'Only once, it was years ago. My cousins were here and we were allowed to go up and play. There was a chest full of dressing up clothes and we acted out a game. My cousin reckoned the house was haunted, but I can see she was just trying to frighten me because I was younger. Although...' she let the sentence trail off, her mind drifting away again.

Elise didn't like to think about a box of smelly old clothes, unknown material touching her skin. She screwed her face up.

'I'm sorry love, I didn't mean to scare you.'

'I'm not scared, it's just you know, the thought of dressing up,' said Elise, a shudder vibrating through her body. Mum didn't quite manage to mask the frown that flitted across her face. 'Do you think the cottage is haunted?' An image of the painting flashed into Elise's head and she pushed it away.

'No, of course not.' Elise wasn't convinced. Mum was always trying to protect her.

'You can tell me you know, I don't believe in ghosts.'

Her mum sighed, the faraway look back again. 'There was something about the place, it was so cold and dingy and I remember being up in that attic and I felt as if I wasn't alone, that's all. Listen to me! I was only a kid. It's natural in an old house like this. Naomi was always trying to frighten me.'

Her eyes flickered down to the floor. 'Look at all this stuff!' She waved her arms at the boxes. 'It's going to take me ages to sort it out. I had no idea Celia was such a hoarder.'

'I'll help you go through it, if you like. It'll give me something to look at.' Elise felt a surge of energy. So many people must have lived here before her, people who were all dead now. How many secrets were lurking inside the ancient bricks?

'Why not start with this? It's a book about the area. See if you can find anything about the cottage in it. I'll take one of the boxes upstairs for you.' Elise took the book and headed off into the garden.

The sky was awash with grey clouds, the sun no longer visible, but Elise felt less of an urge to count away from the small dark rooms of the cottage, her fears subsiding out in the fresh air, school a distant memory. She looked at the book. 'The history of Little Eldon.' It was illustrated with delicately crafted pencil drawings. She flicked through the pages, impatient to see something she recognised. The drawing of Bramble Cottage took her completely by surprise. The artist had captured the cottage and the garden brilliantly. It looked exactly as it did now. *James Tomlinson 1863* was written underneath. She turned the page and saw the heading *Bramble Cottage*. There was a whole paragraph underneath. Her pulse quickened as she started to read.

Bramble Cottage was built in about 1770 by William Darley, a fisherman. The cottage was situated well back from the cliff, but by the early nineteenth century had moved closer to the edge due to cliff erosion. The house remained in the family, but tragedy struck in 1833, when severe storms and violent tides thrashed against the cliff edge and the nearby river flooded the cottage. Virginia Darley was trapped in the kitchen and despite repeatedly calling and ringing the service bell for help, her husband was unable to rescue her.

Maybe Virginia was the girl in the painting? Elise felt cold at the thought. She gazed up at the sky, wondering what thoughts had filled Virginia's head when the river came crashing at her door, crushing the life out of her. She jumped to her feet, suddenly needing to move.

She took the path left of the cottage that led down towards the cliff. The book was in her bag. 'Where did you sit, James Tomlinson?' she said aloud, as she strolled along the path. She wanted to see if she could locate the exact spot from which the artist had made the sketch.

She wove her way along the track until at last the cliff edge was in her sights, counting twenty-five trees before she got there. She stopped and took the book out of her bag, leafing through the pages until she was looking at the picture again. The cottage was further away in the drawing. Five minutes later she stopped, triumphant. The sketch on the page mirrored the sight she was looking at exactly.

Elise stood gazing at the cottage for a few minutes, before a movement caught her eye, jolting her out of her reverie. She squinted across to where she thought she had seen something. Her eyes scanned the landscape. There it was again! A dark figure was walking along the cliff. She hadn't expected to see another soul around here.

It was a boy. He was walking slowly, eyes cast down to the ground, hands shoved deep into his pockets, his shoulders slightly hunched. He raised his head and looked towards the sea, then he lifted his gaze in her direction. A faint stabbing pierced her behind the eyes and she instinctively put her hand up to shield them from the wind. The boy lifted his hand in the air too. Was he waving?

Startled, she moved backwards, setting off quickly home. She didn't want to meet a stranger up here, alone on the desolate cliff. She hurried along the track, her skin colder now and the wind picking up. She ran the last few yards, her breath shallow, sweat beading on her forehead, stumbling along the path until she was in front of the cottage. Not wanting to face the painting again, she ran around to the back gate and let herself into the kitchen.

CHAPTER 2

E lise frowned at herself in the mirror. The t-shirt was alright but the skirt hung down as if whoever had made it had forgotten to put any shape in. Mum did her best, and this skirt wasn't as bad as the last one she'd got her, but every time she thought about pulling up a zip, or fastening a button, a scream lodged itself in the back of her throat. Only old or sick people wore the kind of stuff she wore, despite the young models in the adverts showing off their elasticated waists and 'slip-on' shoes.

She closed the door to Mum's bedroom and crossed into her own. She was glad there was no mirror in her room. It had started to rain, and Elise watched the water sliding down the windows. The gentle drumming on the roof was comforting and she sat cross-legged on the floor, huddled against the radiator, trying to get some feeling into her legs. The loud ticking from the old-fashioned clock on the wall added to the sound of the rain. Ten forty-five, break time at school. Just the thought of it made the panic rise in her throat.

Break was the time that they usually sought her out. She'd tried various different strategies, but they always found her. Her favourite hideaway was the school library, but that last day there had been a year seven event on and she had been asked to leave. They were waiting for her outside.

Meredith was wearing a navy hoodie with 'Fred's Boutique' emblazoned on the back. Mrs Klein had managed to ignore it so far that morning, which was blatantly unfair.

'Hi Elise, we thought you were hiding from us.' That was Meredith. Elise fixed her gaze on the stud above Meredith's lip. It was hard, like her. Elise stayed silent. She'd given up trying to speak to them.

'Her hair looks nice today, doesn't it Cass? Maybe Elise has got herself a boyfriend that she hasn't told us about?' Meredith looked at Cassidy who laughed out loud. Cassidy did whatever Meredith asked.

A bleep from Elise's phone made her jump. She cursed inwardly. Why did it have to go off now?

'You've got a message,' said Meredith. 'You'd better answer it. Don't mind us.'

Elise's heart started racing. She couldn't get her phone out here; one of them would probably grab it. She'd only just changed her number again and she wasn't going to let Meredith get her hands on it.

'What's the matter? Do you want Cass to help you find it?'

Cassidy took a step forward and Elise swung around and pelted off down the corridor, her heart still thumping in her chest. Meredith was shouting at her, but she couldn't make out the words; she didn't want to know what she was saying.

'Slow down, slow down girl.' Mr Greenwood had appeared from nowhere. 'No running in the corridors. You should know that by now.' He peered at her more closely. 'Is everything alright?'

Elise tried to pull herself together, but her hands wouldn't stop shaking. She nodded and walked off as fast as she could without actually breaking into a run. When she reached the end of the corridor, she allowed herself a quick glance over her shoulder. There was no sign of Meredith and the others. The lesson bell was ringing now and with it came a burst of purposeful activity, as staff and students started to make their way back into lessons.

Elise walked in the opposite direction. She followed a lunch time supervisor towards reception. There was a bit of a commotion at the gate, Kelly Watson arguing with Miss Brimmer about her human rights again and why she should be allowed to wear giant hoop earrings at school. As Miss Brimmer frogmarched Kelly into school, Elise slipped behind her narrow back and out of the school gate. Then she was running, breathing freely, putting as much distance between herself and Meredith as possible.

That was the last time Elise had been to school that term. She had bunked off the last few days, the weather on her side, enabling her to spend most of that last week down by the river, walking and writing in her journal. Now she was safely away from Essex and school, and she didn't want to ever have to go back.

Remembering school made her want to count, but she was trying not to. She unfurled her hands, easing the tension out. There was a mark in the centre of her palm, It was a blue smudge, like a bruise, just beneath the surface of her skin. She held her hand up to the light. What was it? She scratched at it, making it fade away then spring back. It itched like mad. Great. She was twitchy enough without some new irritation.

Mum had left one of Aunt Celia's boxes in the bedroom,

and she knelt down beside it and peered inside. Specks of dust flew into the air, tickling her nose, as she pulled at a book which was peeping out from underneath the pile of papers.

It was an exercise book dated March 1892. Elise's breath caught in her throat at having such a fragile old item in her hands. The pages were delicate and torn at the edges so she laid it carefully on her lap.

Elise pored over the faded black ink, the handwriting a string of elaborate loops and curls, making it incredibly hard to read. The light in the room was dingy, the dark sky outside not helping. She reached across to switch on her bedside lamp, moving closer to the light in an effort to make out the tiny words on the page.

Mary's journal
MARCH 1st 1892

Life as a newly wedded woman is quite enchanting. Each morning Arthur leaves for the office and I throw myself into the task of making sure every corner of this delightful little cottage is beautifully kept. Arthur jokes that I will soon tire of such domestic duties but I know that I never will. And today, more than any other day I know for sure that I will never want for anything, for today my life's desire has come true – I am with child.

The signs have been with me for a week now, absence of my monthly bleeding, an inability to face my normally longed for porridge in the morning and a tiresome nausea which renders me quite unable to eat. All these little changes in just seven days, but I know. I haven't told Arthur yet, I would like to keep this sweet knowledge to myself for a while, get used to being with my baby, for I love her already. Her, yes, I know she is a girl, I feel it in my heart. I will wait until the weekend before I tell him, so until then I will keep my secret.

Elise flicked through pages detailing Arthur's business, eager to know more about Mary. The next entry that caught her attention came much later, in November.

NOVEMBER 7th 1892

My darling daughter was born two days ago in the early hours of November 5th. The pain was far worse than I expected but I would do it a thousand times over for my little Annie. She has big black button eyes and a shock of dark hair, with perfect tiny little fingers which stretch out to me whenever I lean over her. Arthur is beside himself with joy, although he was deeply distressed that he was prevented from returning home until the day after her birth.

He was in Brampton, intending to return home after lunch as he knew my time was due. Unfortunately, late in the morning a storm began, the wind roared over the sea, picking it up and bringing it higher than it has been for a long time. The rain threw itself down out of the sky and onto the cottage, so badly that I fear more damage will have been done to the cliff. Thunder started at teatime with lightning creeping up behind it and I must have been hallucinating, as a bolt of lightning appeared to strike the room as Annie made her first appearance in the world. Her cries were so loud I do believe she was trying to match the thunder! Arthur was forced to stay in town until the following morning when he set off at dawn and arrived home to greet his daughter. I cannot tear my eyes from her but she is sleeping now and I must too, else I will not have the strength I need to care for her properly.

Elise stopped reading, overcome with a surge of excitement. Mary must have been feverish and delirious with pain. Imagine if the lightning had really hit the house, would mother and baby have survived? Thrilling also was the fact that Annie was born on November 5th, the same day as she was!

She put the book to one side and returned to the box, eager to see what else she could find out about Mary and Annie.

An old brown envelope, torn and discoloured, lay on top of a pile of newspaper cuttings. It was unsealed, and to her delight she discovered a handful of photographs.

They were very old, almost brown, all taken in the garden of the cottage. The last but one photograph was face down, the same black spidery writing crawling across the back of the picture. *Annie at Bramble Cottage, 1902.*

Elise turned the photo and looked at a little girl with a black cat on her lap. Her face was partly obscured as she looked down at the cat, a long tress of hair falling in front of her face. Elise pushed her own hair back behind her ear. Something about the photo bothered her. She stared hard at the girl's face, her heavy eyebrows and her pale complexion. She wasn't exactly pretty, but she had dark, interesting features. She turned to the last photograph. It was the girl again, a couple of years older now, standing under the willow tree, the same one that stood at the end of the cottage garden today. She looked directly at the camera. Her hair was swept to one side, held in place by a large grip. Exactly how Elise wore her hair at school. As she looked into the girl's eyes Elise felt a jolt of recognition and a pain in her pupils caused her to cry out loud. She lifted her hand to her mouth, her breath hot in her palm. It was the girl from the painting, and it was like looking at her own reflection.

'Hello Annie,' she said, and the girl in the photograph opened her grey eyes wide and whispered back:

'Elise. At last! I thought you were never going to come.'

CHAPTER 3

Elise sat down at the table. Her hands formed a circle around the coke can. It was icy cold, and she enjoyed the burning sensation on her fingers, before pealing the ring pull off with a satisfying clunk.

A couple of girls were giggling at the magazine rack, bodies pressed lazily against one another. Elise hunched over the table, not wanting to draw attention to herself. She was trying, and failing not to think about the photograph. She pressed her fingertips around her eyes to ease the tingling sensation which had remained with her since then. She hoped Mum wouldn't take forever to finish the shopping.

More teenagers walked past, boys this time, shouting loudly at one another. She looked away from them. A poster for a fluffy cake on the wall opposite gave her something to look at. She fixed her attention on the words, and started counting the letters. It didn't take long. She was just about to count them again when the girl appeared.

Elise noticed her immediately. She was one of those effortlessly cool girls who reminded Elise that everything she did was wrong. Tall, slim, maybe year nine, wearing her school uniform like a model; white shirt, black blazer, orange tie and DM boots with orange laces.

Elise stared, admiring the smoky dark shades painted

expertly around the girl's eyes, watching her raise a slender hand to brush her long blonde hair away from her face. She sensed Elise's gaze and looked over at her. Elise didn't want the girl to see her, take in her shapeless jumper and out of control hair, see those eyes gloss over and the perfect mouth twist into a smirk. Too late, the second it would have taken to look away had passed and their gaze met.

The girl's eyes flashed, a charge of white shocked straight through into Elise, and sounds exploded in her head. The pain was incredible, a sharp arrow firing through her pupils, a kaleidoscope of crystals splitting into an image. The shape of a boy shimmered into her sight. A voice spoke in her head, a girl's voice, clear, fierce.

I'll kill Will for not turning up!

Elise was unable to move. Will? The voice spoke again.

How does she know Will's name? Can she see what I'm thinking?

The image of the boy blurred at the edges, then faded away, but the girl's voice was still there.

Elise had to count, it was the only way to disconnect her thoughts from the girl's, but it was hard to maintain a rhythm with the unfamiliar voice inside her mind, and the lump of fear that was lodged in her chest.

Why is she counting? How do I stop this? I have to break this stare.

The girl closed her eyes for a slow second and in silent

agreement Elise did the same. The pictures disappeared, and when she lifted her lids again the girl had gone. Elise sat very still. She had seen exactly what the girl was thinking, and she had heard her voice. But how could that possibly be?

She placed her palms down on the table in an attempt to stop the tremor, which began in her hands then slowly spread the length of her body. She longed to press her forehead down on the cold, dark wood. Drops of water still glistened on the coke can in front of her, and she held it to her forehead in an attempt to calm herself down. What the hell was going on?

Elise glanced around, calming down as she realised that nobody was paying any attention to her. Had her anxiety levels got so high that she was finally losing her mind? She counted backwards from five hundred, each count drowning out the beats of her heart.

She took her compact mirror out of her bag and gazed at her reflection. There was definitely something wrong with her eyes. They looked like they always did, but the prickling sensation around the irises was not anything she'd experienced before. She rubbed her fingertips around the sockets to soothe them.

Elise closed the compact and dropped it back in her bag. She looked down at her hands, which still trembled slightly. The dark mark on her left palm was still there, a blue mark under the skin – a circle, a perfect circle. It was throbbing.

Mum was coming towards her, pushing a loaded trolley.

'Let's get out of here,' said Elise, shoving her chair back. Mum gave her a curious look.

'Are you alright love?'

Elise didn't answer, instead she hurried on ahead, scanning the car park for a glimpse of the girl, but all she could see were rows of cars.

As she eased herself into the passenger seat she pulled her bag onto her lap and held her breath. Mum didn't always notice if she was in one of her busy moods. This wasn't one of those times. She flinched as the crunch of mum's seat belt fastening ground into her head.

'Come on Elise, you know you have to.' Mum's eyes were focused pointedly on her lap.

Elise clutched the bag tighter to her. Mum pulled at the end of the belt which was hanging from the seat, her eyebrows raised. The metal end caught the light and glinted at her, making her mouth feel dry. She closed her eyes, trying to contain the panic that was rising in her.

'Keep your eyes closed,' Mum said, and she felt her mother's arms around her narrow waist, deft, practised at strapping her in, her hair brushing against her cheek. She held her arms rigid at her side, the beat in her chest increasing. She counted each pulse in her head, vaguely aware that Mum was putting the car into gear, the car moving now, away from the supermarket, and away from the girl.

Elise stared out of the window, flashes of fields briefly illuminated under the infrequent streetlights. One, two, three, four, she counted each car that went past. Two pairs of eyes loomed in her head, first those of the girl in the photograph and now the large green eyes of this unknown girl compelling her with her gaze. It didn't seem in any way possible, but the girl's voice had been loud and clear in her head, in the same way that the girl in the photograph had spoken to her. She had to see the supermarket girl again. That was the only way to find out. Her head buzzed with concentration.

'Elise!'

'What?' Mum's voice was knocking against her thumping

head. She rubbed her eyes, scared to lose count.

'I'm talking to you!'

One hundred. She forced the numbers out of her head and shifted in the seat so that she was looking at Mum. The belt cut into her waist as she turned and she grimaced as an image of the metal buckle flashed through her mind. Mum's mouth was set in a line, her face scrunched up as she peered through the rain that was splattering down on the windscreen.

'Are you having a bad day?'

Elise looked away. She couldn't bear it when Mum tried to understand. She didn't get it herself, so what was she supposed to say? She'd missed several cars and had to start her count again. Once she'd reached one hundred it was safe to speak.

'What's the name of the local school?' she asked.

Mum sighed. 'St Saviour's I think.'

Maybe that would be a way of tracking the girl down. Elise gripped the sides of her seat.

'Have you decided what to do about the cottage yet? Are we going to have to move here?'

Mum shot a glance at her daughter, her eyes pensive. 'No of course not! Well, not straight away anyway. We need time to see how we like it here, discover what the area is like. It will be very different from London you know, but I thought that might suit you.' She looked at Elise, who could read the question in Mum's eyes as they probed, willing her to talk about London, about school, about why she refused to go in. She clenched her fists tight, until at last Mum's shoulders slumped and she was once again staring straight ahead at the road. 'I'm going to concentrate on clearing the cottage out to start with. Is it the idea of moving that's worrying you?'

Elise shrugged, turning her glance back to the road. The cottage spooked her. And now this business with the girl.

Mum pulled the car into the secluded space alongside the front garden. The whole area was in darkness, apart from the dim lamp hanging in the porch outside the front door, creaking in the wind. Elise's feet were rooted to the ground, reluctant to move.

'Come on, Elise, you'll get cold out there. Help me with the bags!' Elise picked up a carrier bag full of vegetables, watching her mum as she struggled with the key. She waited until Mum flicked the light switch on and the hall was filled with a yellow glow before following her in. Elise stood still, her pulse rising at the thought of the painting. She took a deep breath then walked briskly into the house, averting her eyes from the wall. As she stepped onto the patterned tiles, she focused her attention on the shapes and colours, the lines between each one, beginning to count her way towards the living room door. But she couldn't escape the feel of the girl's eyes on her, the panic which rose from the depths of her stomach, and the icy draft which swept in behind her and seized hold of her, causing her to freeze on the spot. It was only the force of the frozen gale slamming the door shut which made her bolt into the sitting room and drop the bag of vegetables on the floor, as she collapsed to the floor and cradled her head in her arms.

CHAPTER 4

'Y̶ou're not from around here are you poppet?' said the round smiley lady behind the counter in the newsagents. Elise shook her head. *People down here are so friendly!* The grumpy old shopkeeper from the corner shop back home scrutinised her every move whenever she went in his shop. She paid for her water. 'Could you tell me where the library is please?' she asked.

'Just carry on to the end of the High Street. You can't miss it.'

As Elise left the shop a movement caught her eye. A familiar figure was crossing the road. It was the boy from the cliff; she was convinced of it, he had the same loping walk. He was only in her sights for a second before he vanished.

Eldon library was fairly empty with just a few old ladies browsing the shelves, a couple people were surfing the internet. Elise followed the signs to the reference area upstairs. The librarian directed her towards the local history section, but there were only two books and neither of them made any reference to Bramble Cottage. Disappointed, she went back to the counter.

'Did you have any luck?' asked the librarian; the tag hanging around her neck announced that her name was Sheila.

Elise shook her head. 'Maybe I can help?' she said. 'I've lived here all my life and I do like a bit of local history.'

'Really?' said Elise eagerly. 'My mum has inherited Bramble Cottage and we're trying to find out more about its history.'

'Bramble Cottage?' A shadow crossed over Sheila's face.

'It's on its own, near the cliff edge,' said Elise.

'Oh I know where it is alright. My mother and grandmother both used to work up at Gorse Hall. It's a stately home, not far from where you are. There was some connection between Bramble Cottage and the Big House.'

'The big house?'

'That's what they called it in those days, some of the older folk around here still do.' Sheila twirled the chain of her name badge through her fingers. 'I'm afraid I can't really help you dear. Mum won't talk about the place. She nearly bit my head off when I asked her once, said terrible things had happened there and refused to say any more about it. I can show you what we've got here though. Have you thought of trying the local newspapers?'

'Do you have them?'

'Of course! We have the local Eldon Gazette from 1820 onwards. It's on microfiche, you'll probably think it's very old fashioned, but it does the job! I can show you how to use it. Do you have any idea of the dates you are looking for?'

Elise thought back to the diary. '1850s maybe, that kind of time.' Sheila seated her at an ancient looking machine and showed her how to scroll through the documents.

'I'll leave you to it,' she said, 'but I'm over here if you have any questions.'

Elise read about the stormy weather, emergency measures to secure the cliff and protect the cottage, as well as a detailed account of the drowning of Virginia Darley. She made careful notes as she went along. She felt grown up, like a proper student.

It was twelve thirty. She inserted the next microfiche and

started scrolling through the events of the nineteenth century.

'Closing in ten minutes,' Sheila's voice rang out through the library, making Elise jump. She glanced at the clock. *Damn!* As she started to put her things away a cough just behind her broke into her thoughts.

She jumped, the book clattering to the floor as she turned round to find herself looking into the eyes of a boy of about her age. She only had time to register the good looks of the boy from the cliff when a pain shot through her eyes. She covered them with her hand.

'Are you OK?' he asked, frowning. He stooped down to pick up her book. 'What's wrong?'

She kept her eyes fixed on her bag, scared to look back at him. For in that instant before the pain it had happened again. A picture had shimmered between them.

His name was Jack. He told her this as they walked down the stairs together, out of the library and into the street. She was flustered by his sudden appearance and the faint throbbing behind her eyes. There was clearly something very wrong with her. Surely she couldn't have known what he was thinking?

He stopped when they got to the bottom of the stairs. He pulled a pair of shades down over his eyes.

'You don't live here do you?' he asked. His voice was low and gravelly, lilted with a local accent. She shook her head. 'I knew it, as soon as I saw you. Strangers stand out in this town, everybody knows everybody.'

'So is this morning the first time you've seen me?'

'Of course.' She was sure he was frowning behind the shades.

'We're on holiday, staying in Bramble Cottage – it's up on the cliff over there.' She pointed vaguely in the direction of the way she had walked into town. She watched his face closely for signs of recognition, but the dark glasses were blocking his eyes.

'Who's we?'

'Me and my mum.'

He handed the library book back to her. 'Is this for a homework project?'

She shook her head. 'The cottage we're staying in, my mum inherited it.' She shrugged. 'I'm interested in finding out some of its history – there are rumours of mysterious things that happened there.'

'Ghosts?' he said, grinning. He had a cute smile. She pulled a face. 'How long are you staying?'

'All summer. Look, I need to get going now. Thanks for your help.' She shoved the book down into her bag, and shuffled from one foot to another.

He tilted his head to one side. 'OK,' he said drawing the word out, 'but aren't you going to tell me your name?'

'Elise,' she said. The sun was bright now, and she lifted her hand to shade her eyes.

'Elise,' he repeated. His grin was lopsided. She liked the way he said her name. 'What's that?' He reached out for her hand, but she pulled it away before he could touch her.

'I don't know,' she said. She unfurled her palm. They both stared at the mark. She sensed his body go rigid beside her.

'It's nothing,' she said, puzzled, pulling the sleeves of her jumper down over her hands. She clenched her fists tightly. He was pressing his lips together.

'Got to go,' he said. 'See you around.' He turned and walked off in the opposite direction. She watched him leave, his shoulders determined, as if he couldn't wait to get away from her. The mark had something to do with what was happening to her, both with the girl in the supermarket and with Jack, she was convinced of it. She set off in search of the school.

CHAPTER 5

S t Saviour's school wasn't difficult to find. Elise had gone into the sweet shop and asked for directions. Ten minutes later she was standing at the end of the long drive. The building was grey and old looking, making her feel tired. Pinpricks of pain were starting up in her head again. A small churchyard nestled snugly at the end of the drive. She sat on a bench and pulled out her mobile. She opened a game and spent the next half hour playing, keeping one eye on the school gate.

At exactly three-fifteen the jangling of a bell rang out into the stillness of the churchyard. Elise turned her attention to the gates. Screams and yells erupted into the air and a group of girls and boys came hurtling out of the gate, disappearing off towards the town. There was a constant stream of students after that, cars that had been idling at the road side turned on their engines, stopping to pick up passengers, doors slamming and goodbyes shouted out into the street. Elise tried not to look as if she was staring, although her eyes strained as she peered at every student who passed her.

The girl was one of the last to appear. She was alone, pausing as she emerged from the gate to pull some earbuds out of her pocket and plug them into her ears. Elise put her head down over her phone as the girl walked past her, so close that she could pick up the rosy scent of her perfume. Elise waited a moment, letting her get a little ahead, then set off behind her.

The girl walked slowly out of the churchyard, along the road, concentrating on her music. She stopped to wait at the traffic lights and Elise lingered a few feet away, keeping her in her sights. The lights turned green and the girl sauntered across, her hands in her pockets. Her long blonde hair hung down her back, perfectly straight.

'*What am I doing?*' thought Elise. She didn't even know the area. The girl would probably walk miles and then she'd lose her and she'd have to ring her mum to come and rescue her. She was so engrossed in this train of thought that she didn't notice that the girl had stopped and turned around until it was too late.

The light reflected off her shades. She was wearing a dark pink lipstick.

'Why are you following me?'

Elise looked around her, panicking. She wanted to disappear.

'Yes I am talking to you. I've seen you before, haven't I? Surely you can't have forgotten?'

Elise bit her lip. Despite the glasses she knew the girl was staring at her.

'Of course not,' said Elise, looking down at the road.

'Why won't you look at me?'

Elise dragged her eyes back up to her face. The sun bounced off the shades in a flash of green. She was waiting for Elise to answer, her head tilted to one side.

'I saw... I don't know... '

'Shall I help you?' With a swift, graceful motion of her hand, the girl removed her shades. Elise sensed danger but she had no time to turn away. The girl's aquamarine eyes pierced into hers and despite the flash of pain Elise looked back.

What's happening? I'm frightened and my head hurts.

I was right about the other day in the supermarket. I did read her mind. She doesn't know what's happening either. It must be new for her too. It hurts her more than it does me.

This is not normal. What's going on?

I wonder why it only happens with certain people.

So it's happened to her before! Is she a witch? She's cool though. Ow . . .

'Ow!' Elise yelled, clutching her head. The girl held out her hand to steady her. With the other she dropped her shades back over her eyes.

'Sorry, but I had to do that.'

'What's going on?' Elise whispered. The throbbing was receding.

'I don't know,' she said, 'but I'm definitely not a witch. My name's Grace.' She took a firm hold of Elise's arm. 'Come on, we need to talk.'

Grace led her along the road and Elise stumbled behind her, too dazed to refuse. She turned into the front gate of a small terraced house and strode up the path. She inserted her key into the lock on the front door and pushed. She led Elise through to the kitchen. A large window looked out over a railway line. A small table was positioned against the wall and Grace threw her bag onto it.

'I'll stick the kettle on,' she said.

Elise stood in the doorway, uncertain. What was she doing

here?

'I think I should go.'

Grace turned around, kettle in hand. 'Look, I know this is weird. And you can leave any time you like. But please don't go right away.'

Elise looked around her. The house was quiet, there didn't seem to be anyone else home. She hovered in the doorway, counting the loud ticks of a clock in the hall.

Grace carried two steaming mugs over to the table and sat down. 'I was looking out for you, you know. I knew we'd have to find each other.'

'Did you?'

Elise perched on the edge of one of the wooden chairs. Grace started laughing. A deep chuckling sound. 'Do you realize how weird this is? I don't even know your name!'

'Elise. And I don't even know where I am.'

'You're not local are you? You don't go to my school – and you've got a funny accent – London, is it?'

'I'm on holiday. Mum's inherited a cottage from her aunt and we're staying there for three weeks. Bramble Cottage, it's up on the cliff.'

'I know it,' she said. 'I've lived here all my life, unfortunately. Let's start at the beginning. When I look at you I can hear – see – whatever – understand your thoughts. Is that what happens to you?'

Elise shifted about on the hard chair, the wood pressing into her spine. 'I don't understand how you can just accept this. It doesn't make sense. Reading other people's minds – because that's what you're saying, doesn't happen in real life. It's impossible.'

'Believe me I've been over and over this, asking myself the same questions. That's why I wanted to see you again. Find out what's happening. But I won't force you. You know where the door is.'

'It's OK, I'll stay,' said Elise gripping the seat of her chair as she tried to keep still.

'Are you sure?'

She nodded.

Grace looked directly at Elise. 'Tell me what you got from my mind.'

Elise looked away.

'Don't be shy,' Grace said, 'there's no point. We need to check that this really is happening, so we know what we're dealing with. Guess I'm not going to have any secrets from you, am I?' She clocked Elise's worried expression. 'Only joking,' she said. 'Man, you're sensitive aren't you?'

Elise sighed. 'Just a bit. ' She thought back to the first time she had seen Grace. 'OK. When I saw you in the supermarket café, you knew that I could see into your mind and you were thinking about someone called Will.' Grace pulled a face. 'Then today you wondered why it only happens with some people. 'But I don't get it, any of it. Why me? Why you? Do you know? I was hoping you'd had this…' she searched for an explanation, '. . . thing, for ages and would have some answers.'

Grace screwed up her forehead. And her eyes, Elise supposed, behind those glasses.

'I think it may have happened once before. I was in the Post Office in town buying some stamps. On my way out I bumped into a woman and dropped my gloves. She picked them up for me and I caught her eyes as I thanked her. They were unusually blue and I knew she was thinking that I was polite for a teenager. Cheek! I nearly went to tell her how disrespectful that was to teenagers and it was then that I realized she hadn't actually spoken.'

'Do you think she knew?'

'She must have done, but she didn't react.'

'When was this?'

'Two weeks ago.'

So recently. 'And what did you think it was?'

She shrugged, pursing up her mouth. 'I had no idea. I couldn't stop thinking about it. Then I ran into you and I knew it wasn't a coincidence. Something has happened to me but I don't understand it.'

'Have you told anyone?'

She pulled a face. 'No! It sounds crazy. It is crazy! So it's only happened with me?'

Elise nodded, although an image of Jack wearing his shades flashed into her head. She looked away quickly. She didn't want to bring Jack into this. After all, she wasn't one hundred percent convinced that a connection had happened with him.

'It's really painful. A pain shoots through my eyes and they throb afterwards, then that turns into a headache. The first time was with you.'

'The first time? I thought you said I was the only one?'

Elise clapped a hand to her mouth. *The photograph!* But Grace would think she was really mad. That couldn't be connected. The girl in the photograph was dead!

Grace put her hand to her eyes. 'Look, if I take these off you won't be able to hide from me, but I don't want to hurt you. I need to know what you are thinking. We have to tell each other everything. Do you get it? '

Elise sighed. 'Terrified.' But she couldn't tell her about Annie, the photograph. It might scare her off. She stared at Grace's unseeing lenses. 'How is this even possible?'

'I don't know,' said Grace, 'but we're going to find out. We have to.' She drummed her fingers on the desk. 'I have this idea that if we could look at each other for more than a few seconds then we might get some answers, get used to it.'

Elise didn't think she'd ever get used to it. Grace was looking at her, twirling her long hair through her fingers.

'So who lives here with you?'

'My dad. There's just me and him. My mum died when I was little. She had cancer.'

'Oh,' said Elise, looking at her hands, uncertain what to say.

'It's OK. I don't remember her. It's sad, but that's how it's always been.' She sat up. 'Dad and I get on OK, except that he's always at work. He works at the hospital. If I told him about this he'd cart me off to a psychiatrist, he's friends with several. ' She rolled her eyes, her drumming fingers were more insistent now.

'You want to try again, don't you?'

Grace tilted her head to one side. 'We could have a go, as long as you say if you want to stop.'

'OK.'

They both sat very still, looking at one another across the table.

'Are you ready?' asked Grace. Elise nodded. Slowly Grace removed her sunglasses.

Her blue eyes paled, becoming translucent the harder she stared. Elise gritted her teeth to stop herself from crying out as a wave of pain shot through her forehead. She tried to focus on her breath.

I'm scared. Really scared. How do we know what we're messing with? I mustn't let Grace down. I really want us to be friends.

`Try and talk directly to me. Stop worrying about me! I'm scared, but I'm excited too. Aren't you, even just a little bit?`

I guess so. My eyes are prickly

29

Do you want to stop?

No! It's not actually hurting. Not like it did with Annie. Oh no...
Annie? Who the hell is Annie?

*Oh now what have I done? I'm going to have to
count. Five hundred, four hundred and ninety nine, four...*

'Elise, calm down.' Grace took hold of her hand across the table. Elise had to finish counting, but the light touch of Grace's fingers helped.

'Are you OK?' Grace asked eventually. She had put her shades back on. 'Try to get used to not looking at my eyes. Look at my nose or something.'

Elise looked at Grace's nose. It was an ordinary kind of nose, apart from a small mole on the side. A shaky laugh burst out of her mouth.

'So, the counting,' Grace said. 'It's like a nervous thing right? You did it last time as well.'

Elise rubbed her forehead, staring at the table.

'Look' said Grace. 'What makes you think I'm not mad too? I mean, there's this ... mind thing already, that's hardly normal is it?'

'It helps me concentrate. The counting, that is. I do it a lot.' She looked up at Grace. 'I mean really a lot. Sometimes I can't stop.' She looked back down at her hands, twisting her fingers around.

'Maybe I can help you? You never know, this might help, give you something else to concentrate on.'

'I suppose,' Elise said. 'I guess you want to know about Annie?'

'I can't force you, but... how long can you keep it from me?'

Elise nodded. 'I know. It's just...' She placed her hands down on the table and sighed deeply. 'There's this painting hanging in the cottage. A portrait, of a little girl. Something about it bothered me, but I wasn't sure what. Then I was going through some old stuff that had been left in the cottage and I found a photograph. It was the same girl. It's really old. Her name's Annie, it was written on the back.' She closed her eyes, picturing the moment when she had realised why the girl was so familiar. 'And I looked at her, and when I found out her name she seemed so real and I spoke to her, and ...' her voice dropped to a whisper. 'She spoke to me Grace, she really did. I looked into her eyes and she could see me too. She knew my name. She said she'd been expecting me. I got the same terrible pain in my head.' She stared at Grace's unseeing eyes. 'You do believe me don't you? You have to.'

Grace opened her mouth to speak but was interrupted by Elise's mobile ringing below the table. Elise fumbled for her bag.

'I'd better get that,' she said, 'it'll be Mum.' She grimaced. 'She'll be wondering what's happened to me. I said I'd only be half an hour.' She turned away from Grace as she spoke.

'Hi Mum. I'm so sorry. I met someone and... ' She listened again. 'Yes, at the supermarket.' She listened for several moments and then put the phone down, pulling a face.

'I have to go. She's mad at me for going off with a stranger. I tried to tell her you were like, my age but... mind you, if she knew what we had been doing...' another nervous laugh popped out. 'What have we been doing actually?' She stood up, picking up her bag, suddenly anxious again, needing to count.

Grace grabbed her arm. She focused her gaze on Elise's cheek.

'I believe you, OK, Elise. I know you have to go now, but we have to see each other again.'

Elise couldn't keep still, thoughts racing through her head.

Grace picked up a pen from the table. 'Take my number.' She grabbed Elise's hand and wrote the figures in biro on the back of it. Her skin was soft and she wrote easily on Elise's hand. Grace took the pen and she stuck her own hand out. Elise clumsily pressed the pen down, her hand shaking a little.

'Thanks,' Grace said, squeezing her hand as she let it go. She reached up to brush a long strand of hair out of her eyes and Elise caught sight of her palm. She froze on the spot. Grace had the identical round black mark in exactly the same place as she did. The mark that refused to go away.

Chapter 6

Elise glanced out of the bedroom window. Dark streaks of ink were written over the sky. It made her feel edgy, but she didn't understand why. She wasn't cold, but something in the atmosphere was setting her nerves on edge. She sat down on the floor, squeezing herself up against her bed, hugging her knees to her chest for comfort. She looked down at the list she'd been making.

Mind reading
Grace
Jack
Headaches
Very bright eyes
Round mark on hand
Photograph of Annie

There had to be something linking all these strands together. She felt as if she should know what it was. Thinking so much was making her head ache. Maybe she should look at the photograph again.

She jumped up and grabbed the envelope with the photos in, before a yellow blast of lightning from outside the window sent her hurtling back to huddle up against the bed. That was it! Of course! It was the storm that was sending her body into spasms. Since that terrible lightning the other day she could no longer relax, and her eyes hurt. She pulled out the photographs, willing herself to focus on the images to try and shut out the crashing noise of the sea and the searing cracks of thunder. She looked down into Annie's eyes, needing to prove to herself that photographs did not come to life. A huge clap of thunder made her jump in the air and as she raised her eyes to the window an enormous flash of lightning streaked across the sky. She looked back down to the photograph. Everything went very still. Fireworks exploded in her head.

I thought you weren't coming back.

The same thing is happening. Just like it did with Grace. It's stopped hurting though.

Grace?

Another girl I just met. Who are you? What do you want from me?

I'm Annie. But you know that. I knew you were coming as soon as I saw that you had the circle.

The circle?

On your hand. We all have it.

Who is we? Those who have been struck by lightning? You mean — ouch

What is it?

My head. It's started again.

It always hurts at first. This will pass eventually and you will become accustomed to it.

Why are your eyes so bright? It's a black and white photograph, but your eyes are grey, such a light grey.

You've gone beyond the photograph. Don't you understand anything?

No I don't. Please can you tell me? Who is we? Why is this happening to me, and Grace? What's the matter with us?

I need you to help me

Help you how?

You have to release me from the photograph

I don't understand

You will. But be careful Elise. Never trust a boy who has the circle

Elise clutched her head in her hands. Another fork of lightning split through the sky and she understood what had happened to her. She was back under the tree, the lightning hitting her right in the eyes. The ache receded as she took control of her breathing. Slowly her pulse returned to normal. She turned the photograph face down, deliberately out of sight. She only knew one boy around here. And that boy also had the mark on his hand.

Elise had slept well after the storm. On awaking she made her way slowly downstairs, counting the notches in the wood as she went, careful to avoid looking at the painting. It didn't make any difference, the girl with her beseeching eyes loomed large in her head. A sweat was breaking out under her clothes. If counting didn't work, what could she do to guard against her fear?

The smell of burnt toast greeted her as she stepped into the kitchen. Mum had opened the back door and the fresh dampness of the aftermath of the storm assaulted her as she stood by the door, taking in deep gulps of the air. The sky was pale grey, the colour washed away by the rain. Leaves that Mum had carefully raked into piles the day before were swept all over the lawn, as if the wind had deliberately picked them all up and made as much mess as possible. It had sounded angry, that wind.

Mum had filled the quaint old toast rack and Elise sat down at the wooden table. She was hungry, despite her twisting stomach. She placed a slice of toast on her plate and spread it thick with butter from the dish.

'You look tired love. Did the storm keep you awake?' Elise nodded, her mouth full of crumbs. Mum sat down and poured herself a cup of tea. 'My window was rattling against the frame all night. I don't know what's up with the weather round here! I think I'll go into town this morning, now that the rain has stopped. Do you want to come?'

Elise shook her head. The lightning last night had reminded her of when she first arrived, and she wanted to go back to where it happened, retrace her steps. She hadn't been back that way since.

'I'm going for a walk,' she said.

'Well be careful, the ground will be slippery.'

'Mum! I'm not a baby!'

The green wellington boots she found in the cupboard squeaked as she walked, mud squelching underfoot. She welcomed the fresh air, her head clearing the further she went. Yesterday felt as if it hadn't really happened. She thought about Grace. She looked like the kind of girl who wouldn't have been interested in Elise if it wasn't for this thing, or would she? Grace was easy with her, teased her even. Then there was this whole other photograph business. Elise sighed, pushing her hair back from her face. She had brought the book with her, the one by James Tomlinson and this time she was looking for another house he had drawn on page fifty-four, a far grander looking building this time,

Gorse Hall. The house the librarian had referred to. It looked like one of those National Trust places Mum loved to visit, Elise trailing reluctantly along behind her as Mum oohed and aahed her way around. She preferred an old ruined castle with stories hidden inside the broken turrets to a house done up in velvet and kitted out with gleaming furniture.

Elise paused for a moment to slip the bag off her back and take out the book. She flicked to the page with the turned down corner and reminded herself what was written about the house.

Gorse Hall is a country house dating from the 15th and 16th centuries, surrounded by woodland, two miles from the town of Eldon. The house passed to the Grosvener family in the sixteenth century where its first known occupant Bartholomew Grosvener lived with his wife Elizabeth Page. Gorse Hall remained with the Grosveners for centuries, until the owner Gregory died in 1839. His widow lived on until her mysterious death in 1849, following which it was purchased and renovated by a local landowner, Anthony Warrender. Descendants of the Warrenders still reside in the house today.

Elise studied the drawing. The chimney looked familiar, she recalled seeing it that first time she'd walked around here, when she'd ended up sheltering under the tree. Just thinking about it made her shiver. She could never quite remember exactly what had happened to her, except for falling over and imagining all sorts. She continued along the path, retracing her steps until she could see the chimney poking up above the tree, the sound of the sea lapping against the shore a familiar background sound.

At last she branched slightly away from the cliff and turned into a clearing. It was somewhere around here that she'd taken shelter, but the clusters of trees all looked identical now. She walked through to the other side of the clearing and there it was, Gorse Hall. She took the drawing out and looked at it again, moving around until she was in the position the artist would have taken. It was still quite far away, but she didn't need to get any closer, she'd seen all she wanted to. She took a few pictures with her phone, before turning around to make her way back. She'd try and sketch it later.

Over the cliff path a wash of blue was chasing the grey out of the sky, the ground not so soggy now. The oversized boots felt slightly ridiculous. She tramped along, watching the swell of the waves as she went, ready for the first sight of Bramble Cottage as it appeared in her sightline. Thick bushes lined the path, and she pulled her sleeves down over her hands, protecting them from the spiky branches.

The wind blew through the trees causing a whooshing sound, and she stopped a couple of times when she thought she'd heard an animal rustling through the undergrowth. A rabbit perhaps? Mum said she'd seen a couple already. It made a change from the mangy old foxes which were the only animals she ever caught sight of in London.

Halfway back Elise stopped again to take some photographs. The light above the sea was clear, the cottage easily identifiable now. The sound of footsteps behind her made her stop, hand in the air. She glanced quickly over her shoulder, pulling her jacket around her. The footsteps got louder and the sound of a yell made her jump.

'Ouch,' said a familiar voice, and a boy clad in a baggy green parka pushed through the bush, attempting to extricate a thorny branch from his hair.

'Jack!' said Elise, relief turning quickly into confusion. 'What are you doing here?'

'I live in this area,' he said, looking over at her. He was wearing shades again. Why had she put these stupid boots on?

'Where?' she said, 'I thought Bramble Cottage was the only place around here.'

He waved vaguely behind him. 'You wouldn't know it. You're a tourist here, remember.'

What she did remember was the way he'd taken off suddenly the other day. Her hand felt like a weight in her pocket as she curled her fingers around the circle.

'Which way are you heading?'

'Back home,' she said, 'I've been looking for Gorse Hall.'

His head shot up. 'What do you want to go there for?'

His sharp tone surprised her. She took the book out of her bag, her discomfort increasing.

'Look,' she said, 'I really like these drawings. I'm trying to locate where the artist sat when he drew them. I took some photos to compare them.' She shrugged, embarrassed. 'It's something to do.'

He took the book from her, flicking through the pages. He paused momentarily at the one of Gorse Hall, before settling on the picture of Bramble Cottage. 'Show me where this was done.'

They walked a bit further along the path, Elise leading, conscious of his breathing behind her. Once she'd located the exact spot she took out her phone and captured the cottage in a photo. It reminded her of the first time she'd spotted him. 'This is where . . .' she started to say, biting down hard on her lip to stop herself. She'd almost forgotten that he hadn't mentioned seeing her on the cliff. Jack studied the drawing.

'Wow! I can't draw at all.'

'I love drawing.' Her face coloured up. 'Art is my favourite lesson at school.' *Why did she have to say such nerdy things?*

'Could you draw that?' he nodded towards the cottage.

She pulled a face. 'I tried already, but it didn't come out right.'

'Have you got it with you?'

She delved back into her bag and pulled out her sketchpad. She hesitated, then found the sketch she'd worked on the first day she'd arrived at the cottage. It wasn't as bad as she remembered. He crouched down on the floor, studying the lines and shapes she'd scratched across the page. She sat down next to him, despite the dampness of the ground. Dark clouds were chasing each other across the sky.

'It's good,' he said. He flicked through the rest of her sketchbook, 'you can draw alright.' His hands were slender, so close she could make out tiny freckles on his fingers. He closed the sketchbook, resting his hand on his knee. Elise froze, seeing only the dark circle carved into his palm. She was right. Sensing her gaze, he clenched his palm tight. Her insides felt as if they were being squeezed out.

'What is it?' she asked, her voice tiny. 'What's that mark?' She needed him to acknowledge what was going on, reassure her.

'Oh that,' he said scrabbling to his feet, 'my pen was leaking all over the place. It's gone everywhere.' His eyes scanned the sky as he stared out over the cliff. 'I've got to go,' he said, 'rain's coming.' He shoved his hands in his pockets and ran back down the path, his feet heavy in the mud. Elise stared after him. Why was he always running away from her? He was lying, she knew he was. She unclenched her fist and stared at the circle. She traced it with her finger, round and round, and Annie's words flashed through her head. *Never trust a boy who has the circle.*

CHAPTER 7

As soon as she arrived home Elise dialled the number which Grace had tattooed onto her hand, the ink still just about visible. Grace seemed to want to see her too, so she set off straight away for the town centre.

Grace was sitting in the main square. Four benches were positioned around an ancient looking fountain, water trickling feebly out of a cherub's mouth. Its faded inscription was impossible to read. Grace jumped up when she saw Elise. Her shades had white frames this time, but Elise still couldn't help avoiding her eyes.

She hurried towards her.

'Have you found something out? Tell me.' Grace's face was eager to know.

Elise looked down at Grace, the sun glaring off of her shades.

'Not exactly, but . . .'

'Let's walk,' said Grace. 'I can't sit here any more.'

They stood up together and headed away from the town centre. 'We can go down to the river,' said Grace. 'I'll show you the way.'

The riverside was quiet, deserted apart from the odd cyclist wheeling slowly by, and the ducks, silently swimming through the murky green water. 'Let's sit here,' said Grace, pointing to the bank.

'So tell me what's happened,' Grace said, as she stretched out next to Elise.

'I spoke to Annie again.' She explained to Grace about the lightning and the mark on the hand. Grace unfurled her hand and studied the mark. Hers was a perfect circle now, just like Elise's.

'Of course! I was struck by lightning too,' Grace said, shaking her head in disbelief. 'I wasn't quite sure what had happened at the time.'

'Same here. I found out something else, as well,' said Elise, gazing out across the water. Grace waited. 'The thing is, there's something I haven't told you.'

'I knew it!' said Grace, 'I guessed as much the other day. Honestly Elise, you're just making everything harder by keeping stuff back. I'm on your side, you know.'

Elise felt her cheeks burning, the skin on her hand prickling. She scratched at the circle as she spoke.

'I met this boy in the library, his name's Jack.'

Grace screwed her face up. 'What does he look like?'

Elise conjured an image of the boy into her mind. She could feel the heat in her cheeks again. 'He's kind of tall, dark brown hair that falls in front of his eyes, and he's got a very distinctive walk. He's a bit older than us.'

Grace jumped up onto her feet, and started walking along with exaggerated strides, her hands shoved down into make believe pockets. 'Like this?' she asked, looking at Elise.

'That's just how he walks!' Elise said. 'How can you... do you know him?'

Grace sat back down next to Elise, grinning. She shrugged her shoulders. 'Your description, and you forget what a small place this is. It's Jack Warrender. He goes to my school. He's in the sixth form. He's alright actually, bit of a loner. His family are loaded. He lives up at Gorse Hall.'

'Gorse Hall? But that's one of the drawings I've been looking at. It's huge!'

'It's belonged to his family for generations, I think,' said Grace. 'Anyway, enough about his house, what has Jack got to do with this?' She glanced down at her hand as she spoke.

'I don't know, but he's got the same mark as us. And he's really funny about it. When he first saw mine he practically ran away from me, and then the next time when I noticed his and I asked him about it, he said it was ink, a leaking pen.'

Grace laughed. She held her hand out. 'Yeah, right, this is definitely a leaking pen.'

They both stared at the circle. Grace sighed.

'What is it?' asked Elise.

'I was just thinking I wish I could talk about it with Will, but we're not speaking at the moment. He's really good at giving advice. But even if we were speaking, I don't think I could tell him about this.'

'Is Will your boyfriend?'

'Kind of. Well, not at the moment. I think there's someone else...' She plucked at the grass. Elise waited, wanting to know more. Grace looked at her. 'So you said you saw Jack again?'

'Yes.' She explained about the walk. 'I know I've only met him twice, but he seems OK. Although I did get the impression that there was a lot he wasn't telling me. And he definitely didn't tell me he lived at Gorse Hall. He didn't seem to want me to know about that. And I haven't told you what else Annie said. She warned me not to trust any boy with the circle. So that means...' her voice trailed off.

'Jack,' said Grace.

The girls were silent for a moment, watching a dog that was scrabbling about down by the river. The bright green water rippled gently in the breeze.

Grace stood up. 'Obviously he knows a lot more than he's telling us. Have you arranged to meet him again?'

Elise stretched her legs out. 'No,' she said. 'He didn't give me his number or anything.'

'Well we know where he lives,' said Grace. 'And I've always wanted to have a look round Gorse Hall.' She got slowly to her feet. 'Whether you like it or not, we're going to have to talk to Jack about this. He's the only person that can possibly have any answers.'

'Look, I can't go now, I'm meeting Mum at the museum in town. I could meet you tomorrow?

Grace nodded. 'OK, here, about one? We can grab some chips on the way.'

The museum shop was tiny, every inch of space covered with gifts. Racks of postcards, tea towels, pencils, stationery, mugs, all delicately decorated with the rocky skyline of Eldon. Elise was only interested in the bookshelf. She took her phone out of her pocket and texted Mum:

In the museum shop, come here when you finish

She reached up and took a slim hardback from the shelf. *'Little Eldon, the rocky village.'* She hadn't realised the rocks were so famous. The book contained a history of Eldon the town, and Little Eldon, the village where the cottage was, and was filled with photographs and illustrations. Local people talked about the mining industry which had once been the mainstay of the town, and there were details of the geography of different types of rocks and buildings around the village. Excitedly she spotted the name Gorse Hall in the index. Mum appeared at her side as she was browsing through the photographs.

'Look at this, Mum!' she said, pointing to a photograph of the cottage. 'Can we buy this book? It might help me find out what happened.'

'What do you mean, "what happened?"'

She realized that she hadn't told Mum anything about Annie, or Mary and her diary. She didn't want her to know about any of it – yet.

'The history, I mean, things must have happened in the cottage.'

'It's a lovely book,' Sarah said, taking it in her hands and looking for the price on the back.

'Go on then, I'll get it for you.' Elise waited outside while Mum paid for the book.

'I didn't realise Eldon was so famous for the rocks, did you Mum?' she said as they headed towards the car.

'Oh I'm an expert on rocks now that I've been around that museum! The most important thing I've found out is why the weather is so awful down here. Apparently all those magnetic rocks everywhere attract lightning. Have you noticed that? There must have been at least three storms since we arrived already.'

'Really? There's more lightning here than other places?' Elise didn't want to think about another storm. They were in the car now and she focused hard on the windscreen wiper, counting each swipe as it swished in front of her, holding her breath as Mum fastened her seat belt and started the car.

'I listened to one of those audio guides as I went round. The rocks here are special, you know? I found out how Little Eldon is known for the frequent occurrence of electric storms.' Mum's words were marching about in her head. Maybe Jack's family had settled here originally for that very reason.

'I've been thinking about the cottage, love, maybe doing it up a bit and keeping it as a holiday home. What do you think?' She looked at Elise.

The painting loomed like a dark shadow in Elise's head. 'Will you decorate?'

Mum laughed. 'Eventually, yes, but not for a while.' Elise knew she hadn't finished with the painting yet. She thought about the quiet of the cottage. It was easier here than in the city, her mind calmer, despite the strange goings on with Jack and Grace. 'I think I'd like that.' There was a lot more investigating to be done. In spite of all that had been happening, something in the surroundings drew her to the area like a magnetic force.

Later that afternoon Elise sat in the garden under the tree. The sun was hiding behind a cloud, sliding out every now and then, throwing warm rays onto her bare legs and arms. Her notebook lay on the floor beside her, the cover flapping slightly in the gentle breeze, Mary's diary clutched in her other hand.

Half an hour later she closed the diary and placed it down on the grass beside her, pulling out handfuls of grass in frustration. She couldn't help feeling disappointed. So far there were no great revelations from the diary. At first Mary wrote every day, but then the gaps between dates became increasingly long. Annie was a sickly baby, Arthur was away a lot for work and the young wife struggled with long periods in the house alone. She took frequent walks on the cliff; Elise liked these bits, as she could visualise landmarks of the local coastline.

The sun was warmer now and she yawned, stretching out to

lie on her stomach. She propped the book open on the floor and started reading again. She had only scanned a few lines, when her mind snapped open, wide awake now.

February 17th 1893

A visitor called at the cottage this afternoon. I was cleaning out the kitchen cupboards, washing the walls down and polishing the tiles until they sparkled. Annie was sleeping and I was cherishing these moments before she wakes, her mood is bad again these past few nights and neither of us is getting much rest. I had just put some water on to boil, when I noticed a shadow pass by the window, followed by a loud rapping at the door. I wasn't expecting visitors and my first thought was that something had happened to Arthur, but when I opened the door you can imagine my surprise to see Mr Warrender from the Big House. He removed his hat and asked if he might come in. I was all of a fluster; why did the master of the house want to see me? Maybe we had got behind with our rent, but Mr Warrender was smiling. I showed him into the parlour and asked if he would like a drink. He declined and said that he would not take up any more of my time than was necessary (can you imagine, such an important man saying such a thing!). Mr Warrender announced that he had a business proposition for me. In short, his wife is unwell and needs help bringing up her child, a boy, George, and he would like me to come up to the house each day and look after him for her. I would bring Annie with me and he would pay me a modest salary. I said I would have to check with my husband first, but I know Arthur will not stand in my way; he knows I am lonely when he is away for so much of the time; besides I have always wanted to see inside the Big House. Mr Warrender was efficient and polite, nothing like the character portrayed by the malicious tongues that speak about him in the village. There he has the reputation of a tyrant, the Devil even, if folk are to be believed.

Elise sat up, her pulse quickening. Here was a connection between Jack's family and Annie's. The house was still silent so she settled down to read some more.

George is a divine little boy, very serious with dark knowing eyes. He is the same age as Annie, but so much less of a handful. His mother tells me he sleeps all night and has done so since he was tiny. My mood has lifted considerably since I started working for Mrs Warrender. Annie adores George, she follows him around all day long, copies what he does and cries when we have to leave him in the evening. But she is sleeping better now and I am far less tired. I rarely encounter the master of the house.

Mrs Warrender is a lovely woman, but clearly unwell. I am unsure exactly what ails her and it is not my position to ask, but she spends a great deal of time sleeping. On days when she is feeling better she invites me to walk with her out in the grounds, under the warmth of the sunshine. These moments are the highlight of my days and I so enjoy the company of such a charming, gentle woman.

June 17th

Mrs Warrender was not herself today. I only caught a glimpse of her as she came briefly into the nursery, but dark shadows circled her eyes and her cheek was bruised. She is naturally pale, but today I noticed how thin she is and how frail. She would not look me in the eye when I enquired after her health and I cannot help worrying about her for I am grown very fond of her.

The sound of her mum's voice broke into Elise's

concentration, and she gathered her books together and stood up, stretching her legs out to shake away the cramp that had started to settle. She ran upstairs to stash the diary in her room.

CHAPTER 8

'Wow!' Elise came to a sudden halt as they rounded the bend, mesmerized by the magnificent sight that stood before them. 'One family can't possibly live here.'

'I tried to warn you.'

Elise turned full circle, scanning the landscape with her eyes. It was all steep faraway hills and fields. Sheep dotted the green edges and a horse chewed at an overhanging tree branch in the field outside the house. Idyllic, she thought, so unlike London.

A large house stood in front of them. It looked very old, the bricks a warm red colour with dozens of small rectangular windows. Elise could count at least twelve; she tried to imagine how many bedrooms were inside. Several large tubular chimneys stood proudly up on the roof and she could see some outhouses around the side of the building.

'People like us do not live in houses like this,' Grace said.

'Is Jack like us?'

'Well he is in one way.' They were both silent for a moment. 'Do you think he'd be happy if he knew we were here?'

'I have no idea – I hardly know him, remember. As far as he knows I don't know where he lives.'

'But we've made it this far, surely we aren't just going to leave without knocking?'

Grace started to move forwards, towards the imposing front door. Elise reached out to hold her arm, warning her.

'What is it?'

'Have you ever actually spoken to him? Won't he find it a bit random, I mean the two of us turning up together?'

Grace shrugged. 'Who cares?' She looked at Elise's indecisive expression. 'Come on, Elise. We need answers; he'll understand that. And at the moment he's the only person we know who might know more than us.'

Elise nodded slowly. 'I suppose, so. But...' she turned her gaze over to the large wooden front door. She didn't want to tell Grace how important it was to her that she didn't let him down. 'Do we ring the bell? I mean, there might be a butler or something.' Grace stared at her and after a second they both burst out laughing.

'A butler. Seriously? Come on then, I've never met a butler before!'

As they reached the door Elise swallowed hard. A large gilt doorknocker flashed at her.

'Go on then,' Grace was still laughing. 'Let's see this butler.'

Elise pulled her sleeve down over her hand, making sure all her skin was covered, before lifting the doorknocker and dropping it down.

'Nobody will hear that!' Grace said, casting a glance at Elise's hand. Elise shoved it back into her pocket. Grace marched up to the front door and banged the knocker down hard. A robust tapping sound echoed into the cavernous hall behind it. They waited. Elise was aware of the wind whistling through the trees.

There was a grinding sound and the door swung open. Jack stood in front of them.

'Elise,' he said, shooting a rapid glance at Grace. 'What are you doing here?' He pulled a pair of shades out of his pocket and hurriedly put them on. 'And who's this?'

'Erm…' Elise looked at Grace for support. Grace winked behind her shades. She stepped forward and held out her hand.

'Hello Jack, I'm Grace. Don't you recognise me, from St Saviours? This was all my idea. I forced Elise to come here. We need to talk.'

'Talk?' He looked back over his shoulder. 'About what?"

'Come with us and you'll find out.'

After what seemed like ages Jack glanced back into the dark hallway, then reached up and pulled a jacket down from somewhere behind the door. He slung it over his shoulder, grabbed a key from a narrow shelf under an enormous mirror and pulled the door shut behind him.

'Let's walk,' he said. He headed across the lawn, head down, shoving his hands in his pockets.

'Let me speak to him,' Elise hissed to Grace, and ran ahead to keep up with his long strides. 'Jack,' she gasped, 'wait! Let me explain.'

'Why did you come here?' he asked. 'I don't invite people to my house, ever.'

'It's important, Jack. Listen.' She reached out her arm to stop him. He looked down at her hand, then up at her.

'She can read minds too,' she said. 'We need to talk to you.' Jack stopped dead in his tracks. Elise let her hand drop back down to her side; it tingled slightly where she had touched him. Did he feel it too?

Jack looked at Grace and she held out her palm, showing him the dark circle centring the firm skin on the inside of her hand.

'This is where the Lightning came out,' she said. 'I've worked out that it went in through my eyes and out through my hand. That's right isn't it? I read that the bolt usually exits the body close to the ground but I guess I'd fallen over anyway when it hit me in the face. Exactly the same thing happened to Elise. She can't properly remember either. Is that how it happened to you?'

Jack's chest rose and fell, as if he were breathing deeply in and out. Elise stepped forward.

'I'm scared, Jack. I thought you'd want to know about Grace. Can't you understand how this is freaking us out?'

He stood still for a while, before running his hand through his hair. Elise liked the way it flopped down, dead straight over his face. He brushed it aside once more. 'I do want to know, I need to know, but we can't talk here.' He glanced back over his shoulder towards the house.

Grace was shifting from one foot to another. 'There's nobody around,' she said. 'What are you so worried about?'

Elise shot Grace a warning glance. She didn't want Jack to bolt off again, like he had the other day. He was still breathing deeply, his expression pained.

'Are you OK, Jack?' she asked, concerned. He nodded, pulling an inhaler out of his pocket and taking two short puffs.

'Asthma,' he said, 'it's no big deal.' He was frowning though. Elise wished they hadn't come.

'We'll go,' she said, ignoring Grace's irritated facial expression. 'We shouldn't have come, I'm sorry.'

'Stop it, Elise, can't you see we need to talk?' Grace's feet were planted firmly on the ground, her hands on her hips. Elise didn't want to look at Jack; for once she was grateful that he was wearing shades.

His whole body seemed to deflate. 'No, she's right,' he said. His eyes darted from one to the other. 'But we can't talk here, being near the house makes me nervous. ' He gazed over at the imposing structure behind them. Elise wished she could see his expression properly. What was he thinking? 'Let's walk a bit more.'

They tramped across the grass in silence. The land went on for miles. It must all belong to the house. Jack's family had to be seriously rich. Jack stopped eventually, pointing to a wooden bench. 'Let's sit here.'

Jack and Grace sat on opposite ends of the bench, while Elise pulled her sweatshirt out of her bag and laid it on the floor, before sitting down on it, opposite them. Gentle birdsong filtered through the air.

'It's so peaceful here,' she said.

'Very safe to talk,' said Grace, 'unless you're afraid of the birds.' Jack glared at her.

'My dad must never find out that I've been talking to you. You'll understand why when I explain.' Grace rolled her eyes.

'Maybe it's better if I just talk to Elise,' Jack said, getting to his feet. He held himself upright, taut with tension. 'I don't know you after all.'

'No,' said Elise, pulling him gently back down onto the bench. 'Grace will listen, won't you Grace?' She frowned at her. Grace stuck her lip out, but kept quiet.

'Before I tell you, the most important thing to remember is that if ever you meet my dad, or any other man from my family, do not look them in the eyes and make sure you don't let them see the mark on your hand. You'll be in terrible danger if you do. That's why I don't want you here. It's too risky.'

Grace and Elise exchanged glances.

'You're scaring me Jack,' said Elise.

'I wouldn't be telling you any of this if I hadn't come to a decision last night. I've been thinking it over for a while but now that you two are involved, well it's helped me to make up my mind. I need to break away from my family and I want you to help me. But if my dad finds out he will – and I mean this - he will do everything in his power to stop me.'

'Why do you want to break away from your family? As if we're going to help you, without any details!' Grace was openly glaring at him now.

'If you'd just listen for a minute!' Jack pulled his hand through his hair, making it stick out at an angle. 'I'm trying to tell you but you keep butting in.'

The atmosphere was like thick soup between them. Elise breathed deeply, convinced her breath sounded loud and terrifying amidst the silence.

Jack took another pull from his asthma pump, then started to speak.

'We call it The Gift. That means mind-reading. It's something that has been in my family for generations. All this,' he swept his arm around to indicate the land around them, the house, the fields, 'the wealth is because of The Gift.' He spat the word out, a dark expression flitting across his face. 'Not because I come from generations of hard working people, who have sweated and saved and passed the rewards on down to their children, but because of this ability to read minds.'

'I don't get it,' Grace said.

'I don't know exactly when it started, or how, but many many years ago, one of the males in my family got struck by lightning and acquired the Gift. He used it to read minds and manipulate those around him. He used it for his own good.'

'But how did he meet others with the Gift?'

'He didn't initially, that's the thing,' Jack sighed. 'As far as I can tell it all started because of a coincidence. Another male in the family, one of his cousins was also struck and they discovered that if they stared at one another, they could see and hear what the other person was thinking. Not only that, but they could read the minds of others. If they'd been good people then it might not necessarily have been a bad thing. Unfortunately over the years my male ancestors have twisted the minds of anyone in the community to get them to hand over land, wealth, possessions.

That's the result.' He pointed to the house. 'Gorse Hall. I hate it. I despise everything my family stand for.'

Grace shuffled around on the bench. 'I don't get it,' she said. 'To get the Gift a person has to be struck by lightning, right?' Jack nodded. 'So how can so many people in one family be affected? You must be incredibly unlucky.'

Jack laughed bitterly. 'Oh luck has nothing to do with it. Over time once my great great great great or however many it was not really so great grandfathers realized the power of the Gift, he set about creating the perfect conditions to make sure that every male child got struck by lightning. Over the years it's become sacrosanct. Each boy goes through a ritual at some point in the year before his thirteenth birthday, whereby his father ensures he will be struck. Otherwise the Gift will die out.'

'But you can't guarantee lightning!' Grace looked at Elise for support.

'The rock museum,' Elise said slowly. 'That's what Mum found out on her visit – Eldon has more extreme weather than any other place in the country! There have been so many storms since we arrived already – and we haven't been here that long.'

Jack nodded. 'It's never failed, not in the many years that this has been going on for. The perfect conditions have been created. He waved his arms away from the house. There's a force field out there, where magnetic rocks have been arranged, and that's where it happens.'

'So why don't you want us to meet your dad?' Grace asked.

'Because he's just as bad as my grandfather was. Ever since I acquired the Gift, he has been trying to give me training. Mind-bending it's called. For the first twelve months after being struck I'm at my most receptive apparently, and I'm his only son and heir, the last male in the family line.' His mouth twisted as he almost spat the words out. 'He wants to teach me how to use the

Gift to manipulate people. And so far I have refused to do it. But it's been getting harder and harder to resist.'

'Why only men?' Grace asked. 'What about your mum – does she have it too?'

'My mum? No. Not a single female in my family has ever had the Gift. That's why you two are unusual. But you can't read the minds of people who haven't been struck, can you?' Elise thought back to conversations she'd had with Mum, the lady in the library. She hadn't been wearing shades then. She shook her head.

'I thought so,' said Jack. 'It must affect men and women differently. Any male with the Gift can influence the mind of any other person, a bit like hypnosis, whereas a female can only exchange thoughts with those who have the Gift. This is why men can be more dangerous.'

Grace raised her eyebrows at Elise. 'This is so sexist!'

'So where do we fit in? There must be others out there too, who aren't in your family.'

Jack's face darkened. 'That's why I'm so worried about my dad finding out about you. I've heard that on the rare occasions in the past when a female with the Gift has become involved with my family it has had terrible consequences.'

Elise tried not to let the anxiety that was growing inside her show. She had a very bad feeling about Annie, and her warning about a boy with the circle.

'You look white, Elise.' Grace scrambled off the bench to crouch down beside her. 'What is it?'

There was a crackling noise nearby. Jack shot up from the bench, alert.

'Be quiet,' he said, wandering away towards the noise.

Thoughts were racing through Elise's head. This must be what Annie meant – something bad happened to her and it was something to do with Jack's family.

'Take your glasses off,' she whispered to Grace. Grace removed her shades and stared into Elise's eyes.

Don't mention Annie!

Got it!

They both closed their eyes.

'Hello Dad,' Jack said in a very loud voice, making Elise jump. Grace pushed her shades back over her eyes.

'Jack! What are you doing out here?'

The voice was deep and authoritative, just like it's owner, thought Elise, as her eyes took in the presence of the man who was now standing in front of them. He was a big man, clad in khaki green, a long waterproof jacket, with sturdy wellington boots and a broad rimmed hat. A bushy moustache almost entirely covered his lips. The most shocking thing about him, which Elise could not tear her eyes away from once she had got over her surprise, was the large rifle hanging from his belt. Elise had never seen a real live gun before. Grace's sharp intake of breath told her that she had spotted it too.

'Dad,' Jack said, his face frozen, his expression tense.

'This is a surprise to find you out here with two charming young ladies. Aren't you going to introduce me?'

Elise looked at Grace, unable to speak.

Grace scrambled to her feet.

'I'm Grace, and this is Elise.'

The man was still focusing his gaze on Jack who looked away, brushing imaginary bits from his trousers. 'This is my dad,' he said, 'Mr – Miles – Warrender. 'These are my friends from town.'

'From town eh? Not from around here are you?' He fixed his gaze on Elise.

'I'm on holiday,' she stammered. Jack shot her a warning glance and she frowned. Jack's dad was not the sort of man that you could ignore, especially now, with his right hand resting on the gun, his finger stroking the metal.

'Your mother will want to meet your friends,' he said. 'Bring them back to the house to meet her.'

'Thanks for the invitation,' said Grace, jumping to her feet, causing a puff of air to blow into Elise's face, 'but Elise and I need to get back to town, now.' She shoved her hands in her pockets, her stance defiant.

'Of course,' Mr Warrender said, his cold eyes on Grace, 'then come on Saturday. Three o'clock, will that suit you?' With a nod of his head, he turned and strode off, disappearing almost immediately from view behind the nearby trees.

Grace sat back down, a low whistle escaping her mouth. None of them spoke for what seemed like ages. Elise broke the silence. 'Are you OK, Jack?' she said quietly. Jack got up and started pacing up and down.

'Now look what's happened! I didn't want you to meet him.'

'I think it could be useful,' Grace said. 'He doesn't know that we have the Gift.'

Jack stopped in front of a large log and kicked it so hard that bits of bark flew into the air. 'You don't understand,' he said. 'His Gift is really strong, it's better if you stay away from him. He may even be able to sense it. This is exactly what I was afraid of. You should never have come here.' He kicked the log again.

Grace folded her arms across her chest. 'Then we need a plan. You said you wanted us to help you, and we will. Alright Elise?'

Elise's heart was hammering inside her chest, as if trying to escape. She wished she were as far away from here as possible, but she knew that she had no choice. Would Jack ever forgive her for coming here? She nodded. There was no going back now.

CHAPTER 9

Elise was exhausted when she got back to the house. The mind reading had zapped her energy. The walk back from the village had taken forever and her head had started to ache. Wondering about Jack and his father and what he was really like made her feel ill.

Elise was still thinking as she rounded the corner and the cottage appeared in her sights. The lights in the front windows felt more welcoming now. She let herself in through the front door and went into the small sitting room, her eyes focused downwards as she held her breath and counted the floor tiles leading past the painting. Mum was on the sofa, an old trunk open beside her on the floor. It was full of papers.

'What's all this?' asked Elise, pulling her coat off and draping it over the back of a chair as she sat down next to Mum.

'More of Celia's stuff.'

'So what sort of papers are they?'

'Mostly legal documents, the deeds to the cottage, birth and marriage certificates, all Arthur's paperwork too. I'm trying to put it into some sort of order, then I'll ask my solicitor what he wants me to do with it. It's the first time I've had to deal with anything like this.' She looked very serious.

'You're remembering Celia aren't you?'

She nodded. 'She was always my favourite aunt, although I didn't see her as much as I'd have liked. I should have made more time when I was younger but life got in the way.' She smiled ruefully. 'I expect most people feel guilty about something when someone dies.' She looked at Elise, her eyes roving over her face. 'Why don't you go and have a rest before dinner. You look worn out.'

Elise stretched. 'I'll go upstairs for a bit, but can I take some of these papers? Did you say there were birth certificates?'

'This pile here. They go back quite a long way. Maybe you could draw up a family tree? That's another thing I've always meant to do. '

'Yeah, maybe.' She picked the pile up from the floor. For once she was grateful for her mum's obsessive attention to detail. She'd have to draw up a list of everything she had gone through so far. That way she would be able to see if there was anything that might possibly be of interest to Mr Warrender.

'You'd better take this, it looks really interesting, but I'll let you read it first.' Her mum was holding out an ancient looking exercise book. The edges of the cover were ripped, as if some sort of animal had been chewing at it, Elise noticed as she took hold of it and went upstairs.

Ten minutes later she was wide-awake again. As soon as she'd started sifting through the papers she realized that she may have found the key to some of the questions she'd been asking about Annie. She looked to the ceiling and thanked the unknown relative who had probably passed on the gene for being obsessively organized to her mum as she realized what was inside the exercise book. Beautiful handwriting filled the ruled lines of the paper with names and dates going back to 1800, underneath the title:

From the Darley Family Bible.

She cast her mind back to the box she'd been through earlier, but had no recollection of a Bible. She ran downstairs, where Mum was finishing the washing up.

'Have you seen a Bible. Mum, amongst Celia's stuff?'

'No love, I don't think so.' She stopped soaping the plate for a moment, tiny lines appearing on her forehead as she concentrated. 'Oh hang on! There were a couple of old books that could have been bibles. Can it wait until tomorrow? I can't remember where I saw them.'

'I suppose so, but can we look in the morning?' Mum nodded and she gave her a quick hug before heading back upstairs.

Elise looked out of the window towards the sea and wondered what Jack was doing right at this exact moment. Why did she keep thinking about him? She hadn't liked the anguished expression which had appeared on his face when Grace was questioning him. Why did she have to be so brutal? She opened the window to let some air in, and listened to the gentle lapping of the waves in the distance and a light breeze stirring the leaves on the trees. The moon was shining down on the field beyond the house creating a ghostly effect. She shivered. She didn't think she believed in ghosts but what was Annie?

A gust of wind startled her and she closed the window. She pulled two large cushions onto the floor, took the diary out from its hiding place and settled down to read. Fearful thoughts trickled in and out of her head. The next diary entry was almost a year later.

April 21st

I cannot stop worrying about Mrs Warrender. She barely sees George any more, she has not the energy to look after his energetic needs. I believe her illness is of the nervous kind, as she jumps at the slightest sound and looks to be afraid. I dare not share my concerns with anyone but yesterday I could not help but notice the dark inky bruises around her wrist. She pulled her sleeves down and sent me away on an unnecessary errand when she saw where I was looking; I know it is not my place to be her confidante but I wish she could speak to someone. The doctor came last week, but Mr Warrender is always at his side and I fear she will not speak freely with her husband there.

Elise wondered how many grandfathers back this Mr Warrender was. She itched to get her hands on the Bible so that she could make a start on the family tree. She yawned. She'd read a little more before going to bed.

She read through the next few pages where Mary talked mostly about her husband and problems he was having with his business. Elise didn't think this was of much interest until the name Warrender cropped up again.

Arthur is not himself lately. I know he has worries on his mind and he does not want to trouble me, but he will never understand that seeing him ill at ease is far worse than not knowing what ails him. Last night we were seated in the parlour, it was an evil night with the wind howling outside and the rain had been falling down for hours. Arthur was drinking whisky, something he does not often do and he suddenly started talking. The cause of his concerns is Mr Warrender, which is why he was loath to include me. Mr Warrender has been meeting with all the landowners in town, the farmers, the smallholders, and slowly he has been buying up their land and now he is almost in possession of the whole town. Arthur suspects there are valuable minerals underground, and Mr Warrender wishes to own the land so that he may start mining it. Arthur does not understand why these men would part with businesses that have been within the family bosom for years. It is money and wealth he is offering, there is nothing else after all, but the farmers will not speak of these transactions, and Arthur fears he is being shunned by men he has known all his life. Yesterday he learned that Mr Warrender has made an appointment to visit Arthur's office, and he is fearful. His business is small and he knows that he will try and persuade him to sell. Arthur fears offending him, plus there is the added complication that I am in his employ. He barely slept last night and went off this morning looking deathly pale.

Elise could barely breathe. She hadn't wanted to believe Grace, but this looked like she was right. Her stomach was churning and she made herself sit very still. Jack's face was back in her head again. She didn't want him to be related to these people, but there was little she could do about it. An uncomfortable feeling was niggling away at her. How much of this did he know? The thoughts were driving her crazy. If she counted back from one thousand that should do it. She only reached nine hundred and fifty before his anxious face reappeared. It was still there when she climbed into bed and it stayed with her as she closed her eyes.

CHAPTER 10

'Speak to me!' Elise stared into the sepia colour of the photograph and focused on the little girl's eyes. Two blank pools stared back. It was like looking at any old ordinary photograph, but Elise knew this one off by heart; the patch of wispy cloud in the right hand corner, the defiant expression on Annie's face. Elise blew an exaggerated sigh out of her mouth and threw the photograph onto the floor. Instantly she regretted it, picked it back up and stroked her finger over Annie's face. 'Please talk, Annie. I want to help you.'

She put the photographs back in the envelope and looked to see what else was in the box. A book that she had glanced through previously caught her attention. She flicked through it again. It was an old book, filled with the smallest print she had ever seen. There was only a tiny section on Eldon, and none of it of any particular interest to Elise. Sighing she was about to set the book down when the back cover caught her attention. It was slightly bulky. Prising her fingers underneath, she pulled out a piece of old fadednewspaper.

FIRE WITNESS DIES
The body of Wilfred Greenman, 78, was found yesterday by a gentleman out walking in Springdale woods. He was alerted to the scene by an excited dog. Police Constable Harris was summoned and arrived at the scene where he declared that Mr

Greenman was deceased. It appears that he had
been bludgeoned around the head with a blunt
instrument. Mr Greenman was the only witness to
the fire which destroyed Bramble Cottage last
week but police refused to say whether the two
events were related.

A prickling sensation covered Elise's skin. She turned the paper over, but an advertisement for hair cream filled most of the page. Who had cut this out and saved it? The only other information was written at the top of the page, Eldon Gazette, 1882. What was this fire? She needed to go back to the library and find out some more.

She pulled herself up off the floor and put the cutting back into the box in which she was keeping everything safe. 'I'll be back,' she promised Annie in her head, 'I haven't finished with you yet.'

'I thought we could watch a DVD tonight. Do you fancy that?' Mum was stirring a pot on the stove and an appetising smell of something spicy was filling the air. Outside, the wind had picked up and was whistling around the cottage. Elise was watching the rain, counting each droplet that hit the window pane. The dark brooding sky made her hands tingle.

'Are you alright, darling?' Mum asked. Elise finished counting and swung round to face her mum. She held her eyes for a moment, but all she could see was the familiar blue eyes filled with concern. 'The film's a good idea,' she said, 'we can turn the sound up loud to drown out the storm.' A crash of thunder made them both jump, and the noise of the rain hammering down on the roof intensified. 'I don't like the thunder, ' she mumbled into her mum's warm shoulder.

'You never used to be frightened of storms,' Mum said, stepping back, her hands resting on Elise's shoulders, looking into her eyes. Elise stepped away from her. 'I know,' she said. 'It's this cottage, I think. The sea, everything. It's kind of spooky.'

Her mum laughed. 'You're right there,' she said. 'Now let me get on with this or I'll never be ready.'

'I'm going to change into my pyjamas,' said Elise, 'then we can snuggle up on the sofa.'

'OK, but this won't be ready for a while yet.'

Elise ran to her room, the noise of the rain intensifying as she went upstairs.

She changed quickly into her favourite pyjamas, which were blue with polar bears all over them. They were made of the softest material and always cheered her up. She pulled her hair back into a ponytail and stuffed her feet into furry slippers. The box caught her eye as she shoved her discarded clothes into the washing basket. She glanced at the clock. Mum would be ages in the kitchen. She had time for a quick look at the photograph again. Her hands trembled as she lifted it out of the envelope and sank down onto her bed. A bolt of lightning lit up the room, and she shot upright, her eyes drawn down to Annie's.

There you are!

Elise felt her whole body relax. She was swimming into those grey eyes, thoughts rushing out of her; so desperate was she for answers.

I've been trying, but you weren't there.

I'm always here, but the conditions have to be right.

What do you mean?

The storm. The lightning brings me to you.

So the lightning is responsible for everything. Jack told me that.

Jack?

A boy I met

Is he a local boy?

He lives at Gorse Hall.
Annie was silent for a moment, but Elise could see her fear.

What is it?

Gorse Hall.

Why does that frighten you?

It's a bad place. Terrible things happen there.

What?

Not now, tell me more about this boy Jack. Does he have the circle?

Yes

Why did you speak with him? Why didn't you heed my warning?

I didn't plan to see him, it just happened.

Did he tell you about his family?

A little.

Ask him more about his family. If he tells you the truth about them then you will understand why you can never trust a Warrender.

I don't think he's a bad person.

How long have you know him?

Well not long, but…

Exactly. But this could work well for us. You have to find out everything you can. Get him to trust you, then he will lead you to the key to setting me free.

Betray him you mean?

Believe me Elise, it's the only way.

Her vision blurred, the shapes of the photograph shifting back into focus. The noise of the rain had lessened a little.

'Elise!' Mum was yelling up the stairs. She scrambled to her feet, holding her hand out to steady herself on the wall. Mum was at the door now. Quickly she put the photograph out of sight. Tiny lights flickered around her eyes.

'Elise?'

She forced herself to smile. 'It's nothing, I stood up too quickly that's all. My head was spinning all over the place. I'm coming now.'

She followed Mum down the stairs. She focused her eyes and concentrated them on the television screen, while her mind spent the next two hours roaming around elsewhere. All she could think about was lightning. And the Gift. And Jack, always Jack.

CHAPTER 11

'Hello, dear.' Sheila was on duty in the library again. 'Still finding out about that cottage are you?' Elise nodded.

'I ran out of time before, so I've come back to carry on where I left off. Can you sort me out with the newspapers again?'

Sheila laughed. 'Of course. You sit down there and I'll be over in a minute.' She pointed to the area where Elise had worked last time. Elise glanced at the clock as she sat down, she had two hours and she intended to read through as much as she could. Once Sheila had reminded her how it operated and she had twiddled the knob to get the screen into focus she delved straight back into the Eldon Gazette. 1880 – that was where she was up to.

The print was small and there were dozens of articles and advertisements crammed onto each page. It was impossible to read absolutely everything so she scanned the headlines of each article, hoping to pick it up that way. If she found nothing she'd just have to come back another day, maybe get Grace to help her. The first headline that jumped out at her said, YOUNG MAN DIES IN FIRE, and her heart picked up speed, but it was in a different village. Her eyes blurred as she scrolled through page after page until large letters jumped off the page at her and she knew that she had found what she was looking for.

MYSTERIOUS FIRE KILLS GIRL
A raging fire swept through Bramble Cottage last

evening, causing the death of a young girl, Annie Elizabeth Darley. The child was left alone in the house while her parents were out. Her father was away on business in Eldon and her mother was up at Gorse Hall, where she is in service to Mr Warrender, the owner of the land on which the cottage is built. Witnesses reported smoke pouring from a downstairs window, spreading rapidly through the house until the whole sky was alight with the flames. The young child would have perished immediately. Several livestock were also destroyed. Neighbours attempted to put out the fire with a hose, but it swept rapidly through the house.

Elise sat back and closed her eyes for a moment, struggling to breathe. In her mind she could see the girl, Annie, holding a cloth against her mouth, desperately trying not to choke. She scrolled forward onto the news of the following day, where she found a further article.

COTTAGE FIRE

Police Constable Harris has been leading the investigation into the fire which killed a young girl last night. Bramble Cottage lies in partial ruins this morning and the residents Mr and Mrs Darley are staying at the local tavern where Frederick and Rosemarie Clifton are looking after the grieving couple, who have lost their only child. So far investigations have not uncovered the cause of the fire, but it was suspected to have been started by the falling of a lamp. The victim Annie Darley was only thirteen years old and it is thought that she was left alone in the house, possibly overturning a lamp. Neighbour Wilfred Greenman who was out taking his dog for an evening walk is the only witness. He was alerted to the fire by the light of the flames which lit up the path on which he was walking. He reports seeing a dark shadow, which he says may have been a man running away from the scene, but cannot rely on his judgement as it was dark and he was in a state of the utmost terror, fearing that the cottage was occupied. Investigations will continue today. Mr and Mrs Darley were unable to be questioned, as their distress is all too great.

A vein was throbbing in Elise's temple. Wilfred Greenman. So this was indeed the fire he had witnessed. Was it suspicious that he'd died so soon after the fire? It alarmed her to see Gorse Hall mentioned in the article, the connections between the hall and the cottage growing all the time. She read on eagerly.

FUNERAL OF FIRE VICTIM HELD
The funeral of Annie Elizabeth Darley who died in the fire at Bramble Cottage last Tuesday was held today. Many villagers stood outside their properties to pay their respects. Mr Darley vowed that he would rebuild the cottage in his daughter's memory, as his family has lived on the site for generations. Indeed it is not the first tragedy to befall the family in this property as Virginia Darley lost her life there in a flood in 1833.

'You look a bit pale dear, are you alright?' Sheila's voice made Elise jump. She blinked back the tears that were gathering along her eyelids.

'Did your Mum ever say anything about a fire at Bramble Cottage?'

'A fire? I don't think so.'

'Someone died,' Elise said. 'And someone else was possibly murdered. Look.' She pointed out the article to the librarian. 'Could you ask your grandmother?'

Sheila straightened up, her eyes wary. 'I told you, she doesn't like to talk about that time. It was a long while ago now. You mustn't let your imagination frighten you.'

'I'm sorry, I forgot,' said Elise, biting her lip. What was it that bothered the old lady so much? 'Can I print this out?'

Elise waited while the librarian printed out the articles for her. Absentmindedly she rubbed the circle on her hand. Every day she felt that she was getting a little bit closer to unravelling the past. And each day she got a little bit more anxious about what she might find.

CHAPTER 12

The drawing room inside Jack's house was enormous. In fact, you couldn't really call it a house, it was more of a manor. Elise hadn't wanted to come, had spent a good deal of the night imagining all kinds of horrors that could have happened there, but Grace was determined.

'Mr Warrender doesn't frighten me. I could try and stare him out,' she said.

'No,' hissed Elise, 'you mustn't.'

'Idiot,' she said, 'as if. But I am intrigued to find out what's going on in his head..'

Elise had stopped walking. 'You sound as if you really mean it. Aren't you scared? I think the whole situation is mad and I can't believe we're going to let it happen. What if his dad suspects something and stares at us? We wouldn't be able to stop him. It's not too late to cancel.'

'You're being overdramatic,' said Grace. 'Why on earth would he suspect anything? We're just friends of Jack – it's simple.'

They continued walking. 'Jack said men have more powers. His dad will probably know just by looking at us.'

'Well in that case, Jack would never have allowed us to come.' Grace took Elise's arm. 'Try and chill out, please. Can't you count your footsteps or something?'

They had almost reached Gorse Hall, the top of the house was visible now above the trees.

'The glasses were a good idea,' said Elise. Grace was wearing a pair of regular glasses, with slightly tinted lenses.

'I picked them up in the chemists. Pretty cool eh? I'll show you next time, we can get you a pair.'

Now that they were actually inside the house Elise couldn't help recalling Grace's words. A maid had shown them in. 'No wonder Jack didn't want us to come,' whispered Grace into Elise's ear. Jack came bounding down the stairs and Elise couldn't help catching her breath at the sight of him. His hair flopped down over his face as usual and today he was wearing tortoiseshell glasses. His light blue jeans were crumpled and he wore a grey sweatshirt, which hung loosely on his lanky frame.

'Dad's not back yet, so let's make the most of it,' he said, leading them over to sit on a large leather sofa, which looked out through wide glass doors on to a lawn. 'You know I didn't want you to come; you're going to have to be careful. Obvious things really, don't look at his eyes whatever you do.'

'How do you manage to avoid looking at him?' Grace asked Jack. 'It must be pretty impossible.'

'He knows I'm uncomfortable with this whole thing, I told him when it happened I wasn't going to have him nosing around in my head. But lately,' he scratched his head, 'I keep catching him looking at me, as if he wants to ask me something. I think he was hoping I'd change my mind but that's never going to happen.' He scowled as a door banged somewhere outside. 'This is him now. Let's get it over with.'

He looked lost for a moment. Elise was surprised by an urge to put her arm around him, but she didn't dare, he was on his feet anyway, fidgeting at the sight of his dad.

'Good afternoon young ladies!' Mr Warrender strode into the room and the girls stood up. He held out his hand to Grace, who was nearest to him. 'Remind me who you are?'

'Grace,' she said.

'Indeed,' he replied, raising his eyebrows, which were like mini broom heads stuck on his face, with little tufts sticking out at all angles. Elise realized what she was looking at and cast her eyes out to the garden instead. A tabby cat sat on the lawn, watching a bird high up on a tree branch, safely out of his reach.

He turned his eyes to Elise. She looked down at the ground, awkward in front of his gaze, felt his eyes probing into her head. 'And you are?'

'Elise,' she replied.

'So you're our holidaymaker! I hope you're enjoying our humble village.'

Elise nodded, still concentrating on the carpet. It was plush and blue. She wondered whether they should have removed their shoes, but Mr Carmichael was wearing heavy boots.

'Don't be shy, dear,' he boomed. 'We're all friends here. Any friend of Jack's is a friend of the Warrenders. My wife will be joining us for tea; she'll be down in a moment. Can you ring the bell Jack?'

Grace and Elise sat down on the sofa. The sun burned brightly through the large glass windows and Grace pulled her tinted glasses on.

The door opened and a maid carried a loaded tray into the room. A thin woman followed her. Her eyes and bearing gave her away as Jack's mother. A smart red dress folded snugly around her narrow frame, and she was carefully made up. She had a ton of foundation over her face and Elise detected a shadow around her eyes, not quite covered by the make up. Her neat red shoes with narrow heels matched the warm shade of her dress perfectly. The woman sensed Elise's gaze and smiled at her. Elise smiled back.

'This is a surprise. I can't remember the last time Jack had friends over. I'm Evelyn.'

Evelyn sat down on an armchair to the right of Elise, who gratefully swivelled around to face her. Mr Warrender was standing with his back to an open brick fireplace. The maid placed the tray down on the table, the cups clattering slightly as her hands trembled at the weight of the ornate teapot and cups. Plates of miniature cakes were piled high and a small bowl was brimming with brown cubes of sugar.

'Help yourself, don't be shy,' said Mr Warrender, making Elise jump. 'You're a nervous little thing aren't you?'

Grace turned her head and shot Elise a warning glance as she reached over to the table and took a plate which she stacked up with three cakes.

'A good appetite, that's what I like to see.'

'So you're on holiday here, Elise?' asked Mr Warrender.

She nodded. 'I'm staying with my Mum in Bramble Cottage for a few weeks.'

'Bramble Cottage indeed.' said Mr Warrender, his eyes narrowing.

Mrs Warrender poured the tea and passed the dainty cups around, her hands still trembling. Mr Warrender's cup was lost in his enormous hands. He drank the tea back in one go.

'So are you staying with old Mrs Farnham?' Mr Warrender addressed Elise. It took her a moment to realize he was talking about Aunt Celia.

'Oh no,' she said, 'Aunt Celia died. She left the cottage to my mum.'

'Mrs Farnham has died!' He pulled at his moustache. 'My solicitor didn't tell me about this!' he said to his wife. 'He knew I'd been talking to Mrs Farnham about the property. Selling up is she, your mum? She won't want an old property like that hanging around her neck.'

'I...I don't know,' Elise said. Her skin was tingling. The same sensation she'd had when she first saw Jack on the cliff in the distance.

A shrill sound from the hall outside broke into the atmosphere, causing Mrs Warrender to jump. Moments later the maid entered the room.

'Telephone, Sir,' she said. Elise half expected her to curtsey. She noticed Grace was smirking into her teacup.

'Excuse me,' said Mr Warrender as he strode out of the room. Elise realised she was holding her breath.

Mrs Warrender's eyes followed her husband as he left the room.

'It's a lovely house,' said Grace.

'Indeed,' she replied, although a shadow crossed her eyes. 'It's been in our family for years. There used to be a lot of farms around the area but they've slowly died out over time.' Her voice trailed away at the end of the sentence and she gazed out of the window.

Elise thought of all the ruined barns and other tumbledown buildings she had noticed on her walks with Jack. The coast was pretty much deserted. Silence descended on the room, noise from the telephone conversation drifting into the room.

'It's very different to London,' Elise said. Mrs Warrender dragged her eyes away from the window. There was a stillness about her.

'Have you been into Eldon much?'

'A few times. I've been to the library, that's where I met Jack.' Her cheeks felt warm as the words escaped from her mouth. Jack wasn't looking at her. 'And we bumped into each other when I was exploring the cliff.'

Was he following me? The thought came from nowhere. She nibbled at the tiny fruit cake on her plate. Grace had finished hers long ago and had drunk two cups of tea.

'Can I use the toilet please?' Grace asked.

'Of course. Do you want the maid to show you?'

'No way,' said Grace, 'I mean no thanks. I'm sure I can get myself there.'

'It's at the end of the corridor,' said Jack, 'turn left and you can't miss it.'

Mr Warrender was still on the phone and for a moment his grating tones interrupted the atmosphere in the room as Grace opened the heavy door, leaving it slightly ajar behind her. Evelyn poured some more tea. Elise could hear snippets of conversation drifting in. Mr Warrender was almost shouting. Mrs Warrender flinched.

'Shut the door will you, Jack. You know your father doesn't like anyone overhearing his business conversations.'

Jack stood up but at that moment his father's voice could be heard clearly.

'Well you'd better find out, hadn't you?' he shouted. 'I'll expect a call tomorrow,' and the sound of the phone slamming into the holder echoed around the hall. Mrs Warrender flinched. Jack had almost reached the door when he froze, looking at something outside.

'Dad!' he called, his voice sounding alarmed. Elise stood up. The door swung open to reveal Grace staring at Mr Warrender, her glasses in her hand. The pair stood facing one another, immobile, and Elise thought her heart would burst out through her chest. Finally Mr Warrender turned, his eyes alighting on Jack, who immediately looked away.

'Well, well, well,' he said, looking through the door, his eyes sweeping across Elise, before turning and walking away, his steps echoing loudly on the tiled floor and ripping through Elise's body.

CHAPTER 13

Elise's heartbeat was pulsing alarmingly in her throat. Jack had been partially blocking her view, but she'd seen the way Grace was standing, eyes locked with Mr Warrender. Now she had a dazed expression on her face and with a flash Elise knew they'd read each others minds. Why hadn't Grace insisted on coming? She'd known it was a bad idea from the start. Just the thought of Mr Warrender made her pulse race.

'What's the matter?' Mrs Warrender looked bewildered. Elise rushed over to Grace and took her arm.

'Grace doesn't feel well, too many cakes,' she said. Jack's face was drawn, ashen. Mrs Warrender looked at them, wringing her hands together.

'Oh dear,' she said. 'Where's Miles? I need to sit down.'

Grace was swaying on her feet. 'My head,' she groaned.

Grace's eyes were closed, her lashes moving slightly, as if she were dreaming. Jack glanced anxiously at his mum, then took Grace's other arm.

They managed to drag her down a corridor and out through a side door, and between them somehow got her onto a bench outside. Jack was breathing deeply, his face grim. 'Grace?' he called to her. Elise knelt down at her side and brushed Grace's hair out of her eyes.

'Jack!' Mrs Warrender's thin voice broke into the silence.

'I'll be straight back,' he said.

Elise's shook Grace's shoulders gently, willing her to open her eyes. Grace's body twitched, then slowly she raised her eyelids, fixing her gaze on Elise. Lightning flashed in her head and pain shot through her eyes, then it was gone. An image of Mr Warrender leapt from Grace's mind to Elise's. Elise could read Grace's fear.

What's happened?

It's all true, everything Jack told us. I didn't want it to be but . . .

A series of images burst into Grace's mind. Mr Warrender as a child, being led by his father into a field, lightning striking him between the eyes. Now Mr Warrender was leading Jack into the same field, going through the same ritual.

But I'm scared Elise. There's only one thing he was interested in and that was Bramble Cottage. His mind is so strong, it was probing through mine, making me tell him things. He asked me about your aunt, when did she die and what was your mum's name, what was she planning to do with the cottage. I wasn't able to hide anything from him.

It's not your fault. Did you find out anything about him?

He's very angry. His solicitor hadn't told him that the owner of Bramble Cottage had died.

Aunt Celia!

`Yes. There's something he needs from the`
`cottage. And Jack, he wants something from`
`him.`

Elise was aware of a hand on her shoulder, gently shaking her. Her gaze unlocked from Grace's. She was tired, her eyes throbbed. Jack was kneeling down beside them.

Grace was sitting up now, her face pale. She put her glasses back on.

Jack took his hands away from Elise's shoulders and she relaxed back. She was sitting beside him on the floor now. The ground was hard under her legs but she didn't want to move.

'What happened Grace?'

'I came out of the bathroom and I dropped my glasses. Next thing I know my eyes are locked onto his.'

'What did you tell him?' Jack was scowling.

'I didn't tell him anything! You're unbelievable. He was trying to find out about Elise, OK. He got some information from me, dragged it out of me, I couldn't help it.' Her voice broke and she looked away.

'Are you sure?'

'Grace is tired, Jack, leave her.'

Grace stood up. 'Let's get out of here.'

Jack walked with them to the gate. He went ahead, his shoulders hunched, yanking the gate open, as if anxious to get them off the premises. He glanced upwards, towards a CCTV camera which pointed down over the drive.

'I'll ring you,' Elise said, as Grace took her by the arm and dragged her off.

'What's the matter?' Elise hurried along behind Grace. 'Slow down. Why are you so off with Jack?'

Grace stopped walking and turned to face Elise.

'Mr Warrender couldn't hide his thoughts from me. He's proud of Jack. He thinks it's only a matter of time before they start working together. I don't believe a word Jack says now. Annie is right, Elise. Jack's a Warrender, and Warrenders can't be trusted.'

CHAPTER 14

Elise was sitting on the front doorstep when she saw a familiar figure approaching. Jack! She jumped to her feet, willing her pulse to stay calm, trying not to count the beats in her head. He pushed his hair back, his shades glinting in the sun.

'I had to come,' he said. 'After what happened yesterday, with Grace and my dad.'

'Grace is OK,' Elise said, 'she rang me this morning.'

Jack was still frowning.

'What's the matter?'

He sighed. 'It's hard to explain.'

'Try. Come around the back.' He followed her down the side path and through the back gate.

'Let's sit down under those trees,' he said.

'Not there,' she said. Wind was pulling the tree branches from side to side. 'Last time I took shelter under a tree I got struck by lightning.' She forced a laugh out but the sight of the tree had made her feel anything but amused. Shivers attacked her arms and legs and she wrapped her arms around her chest.

'What about over here then?' He walked across the lawn. It was even windier there, more exposed, but Elise felt happier away from the oppressive trees. He took off his jacket and spread it out on the lawn for them both to sit on.

Elise looked out across to the cottage. Sitting so close to Jack was stifling her. She picked up a twig and poked it into the ground. 'How do I know I can trust you?'

'You don't, I guess. But we could try getting to know each other better.'

Colour rushed into her cheeks.

He glanced at her then grinned.

'I didn't mean . . . look, I like hanging around with you. I wish I could say the same for Grace but . . .'

She laughed, grateful for his humour.

'Give her a chance, she's on your side you know. We both are.' She hugged her legs to herself.

'I haven't got much choice have I, I mean we're all involved in this now.' His face was serious again. 'Just make sure you're really careful all the time. Try and get some contact lenses, they offer some protection. I'm wearing them now, by the way.'

She recoiled at the thought.

'I couldn't put anything in my eyes.'

'Why not?'

'I just couldn't.' Her heart was beating faster now. She scratched circles into the ground with the twig. The tiny grating noises broke into the silence. Elise reached a decision.

'I've found something in the cottage that relates to the past.' She stood up, throwing the twig down onto the ground. 'I shouldn't be telling you this. Grace will kill me.'

'Elise,' Jack was on his feet now too. 'I don't trust my dad, either. That's why I'm terrified of what happened with Grace. Please, show me what you've found and I'll tell you everything.'

Elise gazed across the lawn. The back door opened and Mum stuck her head out.

'Do you want some lunch, Elise? Oh, who's this?' She quickly wiped the surprise from her face. 'Come in out of the cold and have some nice warm soup.'

The smell of leek and potato soup drifted out as they approached the kitchen. Jack grinned as he stepped through the door.

'That smells great,' he said. 'I'm Jack. I met Elise in the library.'

'Well I'm glad you're here,' said Mum, 'I went a bit mad buying leeks in the market yesterday, and I've made far too much. Pull up a chair.'

Mum turned back to the soup, but Elise couldn't help noticing a little smile that flickered around her lips. Mum bombarded Jack with questions as she stirred the soup in the pan. Colour was returning to his cheeks. Once she'd finished she wiped her hands on her apron and carried two steaming bowls of soup across to the table.

'Is that what you were looking for, Elise?' Mum asked, pointing behind her to an old book on a wooden shelf. Jack watched Elise as she looked to see what her mum was pointing at.

'Is that the Bible?'

Mum picked the book up carefully and showed it to them. The cover had once been red and frayed stringy bits were hanging from the spine, which had broken off in several places.

'It is. What is it you're hoping to find in there?'

'There's a family tree, apparently, although Mary has copied some of it out into her diary.'

'Mary? And what diary?'

'I told you already, Mum,' said Elise, although she knew she hadn't. 'I'll let you look at it some time but I want to finish what I'm doing first.'

'That told me,' Mum said, winking at Jack, placing the book carefully back on the shelf, before coming to sit down next to them with her own plate.

'This soup is delicious, Mrs Martin,' said Jack, mopping his bowl clean with a large chunk of crispy soft white bread.

'Oh please, call me Sarah. Where do you live, Jack?'

Jack glanced briefly at Elise. 'Gorse Hall.'

'Gorse Hall? How strange. Is your name Warrender?'

He nodded, a shadow flitting across his face.

'Then it must have been your father who called me this morning!'

Jack put his spoon down.

'My dad? Why?'

'Don't worry! He wasn't checking up on you! He wants to come around to discuss the property.'

'When is he coming?' said Jack, pushing his bowl away from him.

'Friday afternoon.'

'Do you mean he wants to buy it?' asked Elise. 'I thought you hadn't made any decisions yet. You didn't tell me!'

'No darling, of course I haven't, but there's no harm in talking about it is there? He probably just wants to get to know his neighbours, I doubt he's really interested in the cottage. Now would you like some cake?'

Elise shook her head. 'Maybe later,' she said. 'Shall we go upstairs, Jack?'

'Yeah,' he said, 'and thanks for the soup Mrs, er Sarah. We'll be back for some cake in a bit.'

Elise lowered her voice as they went up the stairs.

'Why would he be interested in our cottage? Is it for the land?'

Jack shook his head. 'There aren't any valuable rocks around here; he had the whole area inspected years ago. Anything valuable had already been moved to the force field. I don't get it. There's got to be something else attracting him to the cottage.'

'What can it be?' They were in Elise's bedroom now, and she squirmed a little at the sight of her favourite old teddy lying on the bed. Jack sank down onto a large cushion on the floor and

Elise retrieved the box that she had been looking at the night before. She sank down next to him, acutely aware of how close his leg was to hers.

'This is the book Mum bought at the museum. Look here,' she flicked through the pages until she found the chapter written about lightning. He read quickly, nodding. 'This confirms what I thought. That's why the land around here is so important.'

She looked up at him and he looked away.

'Careful,' he said, 'the lenses help but I'm afraid to look at you just in case. Which is quite annoying, actually.'

She looked back down at the book, embarrassed. Surely he couldn't be flirting?

'Are you going to tell me what you've found?' he said. His arm brushed against hers, the touch causing her skin to tingle.

'There's a painting in the hall downstairs of a young girl. She used to live here. When I was going through some of Aunt Celia's stuff I found some photographs of the same girl. Her name's Annie. She's a relative. One night when there was a storm outside I was looking at her photograph, staring into her eyes and ...'

'She spoke to you,' Jack interrupted.

'How do you know...?'

'The painting. I sensed something when we passed it. I get this kind of buzzing in my head. It's how I suspected you had the Gift that first time on the cliff. That's why I was worried about you meeting my dad. He senses things. What did she say?'

'She wants me to find out what happened to her. That's what I was trying to find in the old newspapers at the library. She died in a fire here at the cottage.'

'So why haven't you told me before?'

Elise closed her eyes. 'She warned me not to trust a boy with the circle. Then I met you. It's...' she cleared her throat. 'It's your family, Jack, I think whatever happened to her is tied up with your family. Remember you mentioned something had happened in the past with a female with the Gift? Maybe this is it?'

Jack's face was pale. 'Is there anything else you haven't told me?'

'I've read quite a lot of the diary. It belongs to Mary, Annie's mother. She talks about a Mr Warrender. She works for him at the Big House – Gorse Hall.' Her voice was almost a whisper. 'Your family, Jack.'

There was complete stillness in the room. Jack's eyes were dark. He stood up and went over to the window.

'That's what I was trying to say to you earlier, about Grace, now that she's exchanged thoughts with my father I don't know what he's done to her. I wish neither of you had ever got mixed up with my family.'

The wind was sweeping up leaves from in its path, twisting them into dark swirls which battered against the sides of the house. Elise felt the same inside, dark and unsettled, her thoughts churning. Did he wish he'd never met her, too?

'I've told you everything now Jack. I'll show you the diary, the photographs, all of it. And I think I do understand how risky it is mixing with your family, but we can't escape this can we?' Her eyes were like dark pools in her face.

He leant forwards and took her hand. She hesitated, then relaxed. 'No, but we can do our best to fight it. Together.'

CHAPTER 15

Elise stood outside Grace's front door, putting her shades away in her bag before she rang the doorbell. Grace always wore hers. As she reached up to press the bell the door opened, the surprise caused her to jump in the air. A tall man stood looking at her. He had cropped grey hair and a pair of large black glasses perched on the end of his nose. He pushed them up to his eyes and peered down at Elise.

'You don't look like you're selling anything,' he said, 'so I'm guessing you must be a friend of Grace's.'

She nodded, tongue-tied. He looked just like Grace.

'Grace,' he yelled over his shoulder, then opened the door wide and motioned Elise to go inside. 'She's through there,' he pointed his long arm towards the kitchen. 'Sorry to rush off like this but I'm late for work.' He looked at his wristwatch. 'Oh crikey!' he exclaimed and strode off down the road. Elise watched as he fumbled with his keys and then disappeared inside a bashed up looking blue car.

'Elise?'

She spun around to see Grace standing in the hallway.

'So you've met Dad.' She rolled her eyes. 'He's so disorganized. Every day he's late for work. Anyway, come in.'

Elise followed her down the hallway into the small kitchen at the end. A train rumbled past, making all the cups rattle. Grace was wearing a short black skirt, red tshirt and her black DM boots, her hair tied back. She had the glasses on that she'd worn at Gorse House.

'I came to see if you were OK.' The shades gave Grace's eyes a brownish tinge.

'Of course I am. Do you want some tea?'

Elise nodded, looking at the fridge door which was covered in notices. She was tired from spending most of the night unable to sleep, worrying about everything. Jack's visit had unnerved her. She started to count the post it notes on the fridge, most of which said things like,

DON'T FORGET PARENTS EVENING!

COLLECT DRY CLEANING!

'They're Dad's,' Grace interrupted her counting. She closed her eyes and tried to switch her mind off. Grace placed a mug in front of her. 'He never reads them. I organize him most of the time. You look tired.'

Elise sighed, dragging her eyes away from the fridge. Spots of rain were hitting the windows, and a train rattled past, making the mugs on the table tremble. She put her hands around the mug to steady it.

'You get used to the trains,' said Grace. 'I barely notice them now. Did you bring the stuff?'

Elise nodded. 'Just the case, the one I haven't been through yet. We can go through it together. *If* I can concentrate.'

'What's up?'

Elise looked down at her hands, tracing her finger around the circle, symbol of everything that was going round in her mind. It was so hard to put her feelings into words.

'Elise!' She looked up. Grace had her hands on her glasses. 'Would mind reading be easier?'

Elise closed her eyes. Did she want Grace to know how she felt about Jack? He had a hold over her which she didn't understand. But she needed to talk to someone. She looked up.

Elise panicked momentarily as she realised that Grace had already removed her glasses. Grace's pupils appeared to expand as Elise felt the whoosh inside her head.

You didn't give me a choice

I thought it might be easier this way. Just let your thoughts flow.

An image of Jack swam into Elise's head. The way he walked, hunched, worried, as if he was in fear of something. The way he made her feel protective was impossible to put into words. But she cared for him.

`It's perfectly normal to like him, Elise. He's good looking, not my type but . . .`

It's not like that! We get on well, but he can read my mind! It makes everything so difficult. I've never been proper friends with a boy before. And now there's all this business with his dad – you don't trust him, what if you're right? He doesn't trust either – how do I know who to believe? He came over to see me yesterday. I don't want him to be a bad person, I can't believe that he is. What if he can manipulate my mind?

`Perhaps you should stay away from him`

But I can't stop thinking about him

`So you do like him`

Well, a bit

Grace had closed her eyes. Elise did the same and started to count down from one hundred. She gripped the edge of the table as hard as she could.

'Elise!'

She opened her eyes when she got to one. Grace had her shades back on.

'Why do you find it so hard to talk to me? Don't you have friends back in London that you confide in, chat about boys, stuff like that?'

Just thinking about Meredith and the girls at school, the walk into school every morning, her mind full of dread made Elise's stomach contract. She'd been getting in later and later as there were so many things to count, which resulted in umpteen detentions. The long, lonely days before the bell went, rushing home to avoid any confrontations.

'Not really,' she said, looking down at her hands.

'Tell me,' Grace said.

'I don't have any friends. Everyone thinks I'm weird. Some girls in my class found out about my OCD. They think it's funny to torment me. It's not just the counting. I can't tolerate certain metals near me, on my clothes, zips, that kind of thing. It's hard to explain. I hate London, I wish we could stay here. Just meeting you and Jack has been brilliant, that's why I don't want all these complications to spoil it. I'm mad enough as it is without all this.'

Elise felt tears pricking at the back of here eyes and she sniffed them away.

'We won't let them,' said Grace. 'The best thing we can do is get to the bottom of what's going on, then put it behind us. Now let's look at what else is in the case.'

'I'll get it,' Elise said, and got up and went out into the hall.

When she came back Grace was smiling.

'What are you smiling at?'

'You. I think you're fascinating. I'm so glad you came here.'

Elise's mood felt lighter as she placed the old suitcase on the table. Mind reading was certainly helping her open up to Grace. She unclasped the locks. The tan leather was cracked with age. Faded material formed a lining inside the case, which contained a pile of papers, with a bulky looking object placed on top.

'What's this?' She held the piece of material up, squinting at it. Grace got up and switched the light on, as outside it was rapidly turning from day into night. She held the piece of material under the yellow glow. 'It's a tapestry,' she said.

'Not tapestry, embroidery,' said Grace. 'It's incredibly old, look how fragile it is. I'm amazed it hasn't completely rotted away.'

The embroidery was a square of about forty centimetres across, with words sewn onto it. Damp had got to it and the writing, which looked to have originally been in red, had faded. The fusty smell made Grace wrinkle her nose.

'What does it say?' she asked.

FRIENDS FOREVER Elise spelt out the words.

'Wow! I wonder who wrote it?'

'And who was it written to?' added Grace.

'It's kind of weird isn't it – embroidering it like that?' said Elise. Grace shrugged. 'It's probably how they did things in those days.'

'Maybe Mary wrote it for Arthur, her husband?'

Grace pulled a face. 'No, I think someone younger did this. What else is in the case?'

She rummaged around, her hands securing a book, hidden by all the papers.

'A Bible. That's a bit boring.'

'No!' said Elise. 'I brought this along specially to show you.

Mary mentioned a Bible in her diary. There's a family tree inside.' She opened the cover and turned to the first page. 'Look!' she pointed at tiny handwriting which covered the first two pages of the Bible, under the heading Darley Family.

'I wonder who wrote it,' she said. The ink was faded in places, but the names were legible, despite the size of the script. The original writing was dated 1890, and a clumsier, more modern hand had added a few names in, culminating with Thomas and Ellen Darley in 1940.

'They were Great Aunt Celia's parents,' said Elise, 'so that makes them my Great Grandparents.' A lump lodged in her throat and she swallowed hard.

'So are you related to Annie?'

Elise found it hard to speak.'

They both stared at the list. 'There she is. Annie Darley,' Grace read. 'She was Mary's daughter, look this is Mary here, but . . . it's too complicated to work out exactly how you're related.'

'I'll get Mum to have a look.' Elise glowed inside. 'I hadn't realised that I was related to Annie.'

'But the painting,' said Grace.

'What about it? I try not to look at it, it makes me feel odd.' The cold feeling that she experienced whenever she stepped into the hall rose inside her. 'I know I look a bit like her, but I hadn't thought anything of it.'

'I can't believe you, Elise. Of course she's related to you, you look exactly alike.'

Elise felt as if ice was being poured through her body, exactly how she felt when she looked at the painting.

'Surely your mum must have mentioned it?' Grace screwed her forehead in concern. 'You've gone really pale. What's the matter?'

Elise breathed deeply. She couldn't think about the painting now. 'See if there's anything else in the Bible,' she said, looking at the fridge. She needed to count the post-it notes once more.

Grace carefully flicked through the rest of the Bible. 'No. That's a shame.'

'Let me see,' said Elise, taking the book and holding it up to the light. 'The spine looks a bit thick, here, see.' She inserted her long black nails into the top of the spine and poked around for a moment, before extricating a carefully folded piece of paper.

'You have a look first,' said Grace, passing the piece of paper to Elise. 'Careful when you open it, it looks as if it might disintegrate.' Elise unfolded it slowly, the paper cracking and splitting along the folds.

'It's a letter, addressed to Mary. It's handwritten,' she said breathlessly. She was silent for a moment as she devoured the contents of the letter. When she had finished, she was trembling slightly.

'Oh Grace,' she said, 'I think it's from Mrs Warrender – old Mrs Warrender I mean, George's mum.'

'You mean a relative of Jack?' Grace said biting her lip. 'This is so weird. Read it aloud.'

Elise raised her voice as she started reading in order to make herself heard over the rain, which was hammering down hard on the windows, smacking against the glass, then sliding down into little streams. She scratched at her hand, which had started to irritate her. Grace did the same.

Dear Mary,

No doubt you will be surprised to receive a note from me but there is no one else in the household that I can trust, save Betty, who has promised to deliver this letter to you. As a mother yourself I know that you will understand when you discover what motivates me to communicate with you in this way.

My child is in danger. I fear for his life and it is for this reason that

I have no choice but to turn to you.

You will know of late that I have been unwell; in truth it is my husband that drives me to this sickness. I know it is wrong to question a husband's judgment, but I have remained silent for too long, and I must speak out on account of my condition. I am with child, and it is for this reason that I hope something can be done to stop him.

Next month my first-born child, George will reach the age of thirteen. My husband plans to initiate him into a family ritual about which I may not go into detail here. Indeed, it is so fanciful I fear you would not believe a word of it were I to attempt to describe it to you in this letter. Pray trust in me that I speak the truth, I do swear on the life of my child, the only thing I have which gives me any joy in life. My husband wishes to interfere with my child's mind, to take away the goodness that he has in his heart and turn him into a replica of himself. You must have heard the talk in the village, of how Mr Warrender is slowly encroaching on all the land, buying up all the properties. His methods are underhand and unspeakable. He is greedy for wealth and if he is not stopped will soon own all the mining land in the county. With George in his power, this will continue down through another generation and eventually destroy this community.

Please dearest Mary, take heed and have faith in my words. There is a way that my husband can be stopped from corrupting my child, but I need help. Will you help me?

Please come to the house as soon as you can, or send news with Betty. I cannot impress upon you enough how urgent this situation is. George's birth date falls on the last week in September, the 27th; I must speak with you before this date.

Lastly, this letter must only be read by your good self. I fear the consequences were my husband to know what I have written.

God bless you.

'Is it signed?' Grace asked.

Elise shook her head, biting her lip. 'But it fits in with what Mary has written in her diary. She works at Gorse Hall looking after George. And she worries about her employer, Mrs Warrender, who is always ill. It has to be her. She's concerned about George.'

'Have you finished reading the diary?'

'Not yet.' She scratched at her hand as a loud banging at the door made them all jump. 'The rain is coming down hard now,' she said. 'I'd better think about getting home. Mum will be worried.'

'Why don't you stay here?' said Grace, 'you can phone your mum from here.'

Elise was relieved not to have to make the journey home and especially not to see that painting. When she'd finished speaking to Mum Grace came out into the hall.

'I'll just let Dad know. I've made some more tea. Why don't you take it through into the front room? It's warmer in there.'

Elise poured out two mugs of tea and carried them through into the front room. The fire was lit, and she pulled her chair up in front of the cosy glow. Grace came in and sighed as she sat down.

'Dad said Will stopped by when I was out earlier.'

'You still haven't told me about him. He's your boyfriend, right?'

'On and off,' said Grace, pulling a face. 'If we were to mind read now you'd see exactly how confused I am. Me and Will, we go back ages. We've been friends since primary school.'

'So the other day, when I first met you...'

Grace rubbed her face, 'He was supposed to be meeting me to help buy dad a present. He didn't turn up. There's a new girl at school who's after him and we'd had a row about it the day before.'

'How old is Will?'

'Fifteen,' said Grace.

The window was making a clattering noise now, the wind adding to the din.

'So what are you going to do about Jack then?'

She looked down at her hands, remembering his hand on her arm. Did that mean he liked her? It was nothing, surely.

'You really like him don't you?'

She nodded, screwing her face up. 'But I wish you did too. As a friend, I mean.'

'It's not that I don't like him, It's his dad I don't like, and that makes me wary of Jack. He might still be keeping things from us. We won't be able to stop his dad coming to see your mum, you know.'

'Maybe I should tell her what's going on?'

'No! That's too risky. She wouldn't be able to get her head around it and she might stop me seeing you. Then what would we do? We're supposed to be looking for whatever it is we need to find. It's hopeless.'

A ripple of thunder vibrated in the distance. 'The storm's getting closer,' said Grace, scratching her hand. 'My hand hurts, does yours?'

'Yes,' said Elise, absentmindedly scratching the circle, although she felt safer in Grace's house, away from the cottage, which was steeped in history. A beeping noise came from her bag. She took out her phone, read the message. It was from Jack.

Meet in town tomorrow? The Bean Café at 11? Need to talk.

She showed it to Grace. 'Will you come too? I don't know where that is.' She felt safer with Grace around.

Grace nodded. 'Sure, but let him know I'm coming.'

Staying at Grace's tonight, so she's coming too. Hope that's OK. She pressed send.

'I wonder what he wants to talk about.'

'We'll soon find out.'

CHAPTER 16

Elise and Grace were sitting opposite Jack in the cafe. A bell jangled as the door opened and a young couple came in. The girl tightened her grip on the boy's arm as they approached. Grace stiffened as they walked past the table. The girl flicked her hair back over her shoulder as they went past.

'What's the matter Will?' Grace called to the boy. 'Aren't you even going to say hello?'

The boy turned and looked at her, shoving his hands in his pockets, his mouth twisted, uncomfortable.

'Look, Grace,' he started to say, but was stopped by the girl yanking on his arm.

'Come on,' she said. 'Let's go somewhere else. There are far too many people in here.'

Will looked embarrassed as he was dragged off.

Jack turned to look around the café. They were practically the only people in there.

'What was all that about?' he asked.

'Nothing,' snapped Grace. Elise watched the couple walking off down the street. Will looked back over his shoulder at Grace.

'I think he still likes you.'

'I don't care,' said Grace, 'I just don't get what he's doing with that airhead.' She stood up abruptly. 'I'm going to the loo.' She walked away from the café down the street.

'Where…?' Elise got up to follow, but Jack put a hand on her arm to stop her.

'Give her a minute,' he said. 'She's tough, you'll see. I feel sorry for the guy when she gets her hands on him!' Elise sat back down again, staring after Grace. She hadn't planned on being left alone with Jack. 'i want to know what's up with you.'

Elise went for the safest option.

'I'm not happy about Mum, to be honest. I don't like the idea of your dad coming to see her. Do you think I should tell her what's going on?'

'Maybe. Look, when Grace comes back we should decide exactly how much we can tell your mum, and how to make her believe us, that's the most important bit. Otherwise it could backfire on us and we don't want her saying the wrong thing to my dad. He's already suspicious enough as it is. I don't think Grace should go anywhere near him either.'

'She won't disagree with that. Where is she?' asked Elise, looking back down the road in the general direction in which Grace had disappeared. Jack shrugged.

'Stop worrying about Grace. I want to talk to you before she comes back.' Elise kept her eyes firmly on the teabag floating around in her cup.

'What about?'

'I'm worried because my dad has got into her mind. He's very powerful and may have sent her messages that she doesn't even realize yet. That's the only reason I don't quite trust her.'

'But she told me what he said. Can't you try and get on with her, for my sake? It's not her fault he got into her mind. It's just as difficult for her.'

'OK, I'll try, just for you, but only if you promise not to look so worried.'

'Is that why you don't want to let him, what do you call it, 'mind-bend' you?'

He nodded. 'By that he means a series of regular exchanges where he teaches me how to manipulate others. The more time he spends in my mind the greater the control over me he has.'

'It's awful. He's your dad; you can't spend your whole life avoiding him. Unless...' The thought made her feel uncomfortable.

'Unless what?' He rested his elbows on the table and moved closer to her.

'Unless you run away. Properly I mean. But obviously that's not an option.'

'I couldn't leave Mum.'

'Is there anyway of reversing the power?' she asked.

'Not that I know of,' he said, 'if there was that would solve all my problems.'

A shadow fell across the table. It was Grace.

'Where did you get to?' Elise asked, sitting back in her chair, shivering now as the wind had started up again.

'I went to the loo. I said didn't I?'

'Yeah, but you didn't go in the café.'

'I went over to the ones in the square.'

Elise was surprised at Grace's harsh tone. Jack looked from one girl to another, but she looked away. Pinpricks seared through her palm. Maybe it was the bad weather, making Grace cruel, like the wind. She screwed up her fists and concentrated on her rapid heartbeat, counting the beats.

Grace sat down opposite Elise.

'Sorry,' she said. 'Will drives me insane. Just ignore my moods.'

'It's not that,' Elise said. 'I don't know what is true and what isn't, who I can trust. Maybe the whole thing is in our imagination. I think we should go home and speak to Mum. If we warn her about Mr Warrender I expect she'll cancel his visit. Once Mum's made her mind up she's unlikely to change it.' Elise stood up.

'What do you think Grace?' Elise was grateful that Jack was making an effort.

She nodded. 'Good idea,'

'Come on, let's see what time the next bus goes. It's far too muddy to walk back and I think it's going to start raining again soon.' The three of them looked up at the dark clouds gathering overhead. Elise felt as if all their troubles were bundled up in the clouds and any moment now would come pouring down all over them.

CHAPTER 17

Elise stamped her feet up and down, trying to generate some warmth around her body. They had been waiting at least forty-five minutes at the bus stop, the sky getting more threatening by the moment. Grace was pacing to the corner of the road and back, her arms folded around her body to try and keep warm.

'At last!' she said, as the old green bus she had been longing to see appeared in the distance. She walked forward and stuck her arm out in such a way that the driver couldn't miss it. Jack and Elise followed her, Jack's hand lightly on Elise's back as she mounted the steep steps onto the bus. The bus was empty so they made the most of the space on the back seat. Grace wiped the condensation away from the window, but the rain was heavy, obscuring any view from the window.

'I need to get away from here,' she said, 'I'm sick of this countryside, the weather, everything. You don't know how lucky you are, Elise, having somewhere else to call home. You'd be crazy to move down here.' She pressed her nose against the glass, lost in her thoughts. Elise noticed she was scratching furiously at her hand. She removed one of her damp woolly gloves and studied her own hand. The flesh was pink and mottled, cold to the touch, the circle dark and clear in the middle of her palm. The skin inside the circle was extraordinarily white. She reached it across and took Grace's hand. Curious to see whether the circles were exactly the same size, she placed her palm carefully over Grace's and pressed.

Afterwards she was unable to say what had happened next. Everything seemed to occur at once, and very fast. The driver swerved to avoid a man who walked in front of the bus. A huge thunderclap burst through the sky, loud enough to make the bus driver jump in his seat, his hands leaving the steering wheel momentarily, causing the bus to lurch to the side, wheels slipping in the mud and off the path. The window next to Grace shattered, glass splintering into thousands of pieces, most of them missing her apart from one large diamond shaped segment which embedded itself just above her cheekbone, narrowly missing her right eye. Elise heard the shattering of the glass and the screech of the brakes as the driver desperately tried to regain control, but the bolt of electricity which had travelled through their bodies the moment their hands touched was all consuming. Elise started shaking from head to toe, wrenching her hand away from Grace's.

The bus shuddered to a halt. A sound pierced into Elise's mind, jolting her into action. Grace was screaming, her hand to her face, tears of blood streaming down her cheek. The bus had stopped at an awkward angle; it's front wheels no longer on the road.

'Is everyone alright?' the driver was making his way down the bus, unsteady on his feet, clutching at the seats as he lurched towards them. His eyes bulged out of his white face when he caught sight of Grace. He rummaged around in his pockets for his phone, but his hands were shaking so much he dropped it on the floor. Jack swooped down to pick it up. 'Call an ambulance, lad,' he gasped. 'Is anyone else hurt?'

Elise made her way across the aisle, pulling her scarf over her head and using it to wipe the blood away from Grace's face.

'Grace?' Her head rested against the remaining window, her shades twisted and broken on her lap. 'Are you OK?' she asked again, frantically searching Grace's eyes with her own. The familiar spinning started up, her ears roaring, as Grace opened her eyes.

Elise – are you hurt? What happened there? It was another storm, the thunder was loud like it was when I was struck by lightning. It came through the window at me. My head feels funny.

Her eyelids slid down over her eyes, releasing Elise's mind.

'Elise!' Jack's voice was insistent, barely disguising his panic. He was shaking her shoulders again as she came back to him. 'What are you playing at?' he hissed into her ear. Her head span, a mixture of Grace's mind and Jack's harsh words. 'It's OK,' he called to the driver, 'she fainted that's all.' He came back to help her with Grace. He too was shaking. 'I sent the driver away to look for the ambulance.'

'Is it coming?' her voice crackled as she gazed at Grace, who loooked dazed, a dark bruise revealing itself over her cheek, the blood dried black, the turquoise scarf a shock of colour against her white face. The sound of a loud siren answered her question, and she burst into tears. Moments later the narrow aisle of the coach was filled with paramedics and equipment. Police radios crackled into action, competing with the sound of the heavy rain on the roof. Grace was helped outside while a woman who introduced herself as Kathy knelt down beside Elise and Jack and asked them lots of questions. Once she was satisfied they were both unhurt, she led them out of the coach.

'That girl passed out,' the driver was saying. Kathy turned to

Elise.

'You didn't tell me that you lost consciousness,' she said.

'I was dizzy, that's all, seeing all the blood,'

'It looked like she fainted, but she didn't,' Jack added, 'he was confused,' he nodded at the driver, who was mopping his forehead with a large handkerchief, while a paramedic checked his blood pressure. His round stomach was heaving up and down, his breath rattling.

'What's your name, Sir?' the paramedic was asking.

'Mick,' he spluttered. The paramedic spoke to Kathy for a moment, before going back outside.

'We need to take Mick and Grace to hospital,' said Kathy, 'Grace's father will meet us there. We'll double-check you two when we get there, but I think you're all OK. You had a lucky escape, really. The rain makes the roads hazardous – I'm guessing the bus slid on account of the rain.' Two more policemen had arrived on motorcycles and one started checking over the scene while the first made contact with the paramedic. 'The police may want to ask you a few questions,' said Kathy, 'but it's nothing for you to worry about. Our main priority now is getting Grace's eye dressed.'

Kathy supported Grace as she made her way into the ambulance, accompanied by Elise. 'You go with Mick love,' she said to Jack, 'keep him company. His wife is on her way to the hospital, but I've told her she's nothing to worry about.'

Elise phoned her mum from the ambulance, and with a little help from Kathy managed to persuade her that she didn't need to come to the hospital. Grace opened her eyes when they had almost reached their destination.

'How are you feeling?' Elise asked, stroking her friend's forehead. A little colour had filled out her high cheekbones.

'A bit better,' said Grace, but closed her eyes again after that and Kathy took over as they wheeled her out of the ambulance and into the hospital. Jack and Mick arrived while they were waiting in a corridor. Grace was whisked away to have her eye looked at, and shortly after Mick was called into a cubicle.

'Did you ring your mum?' Jack asked. These were the first words he'd spoken since his arrival and she was convinced he was annoyed with her for mind-reading with Grace. Every time she thought about Grace's face covered in blood the nausea returned. She hadn't the strength to argue. She shook her head and closed her eyes.

Unbelievably she dozed off. A male voice awoke her. She started upright, blinking at the vaguely familiar face peering down at her. Thick brown hair sticking out at angles and dark-rimmed spectacles framed a long thin face.

The man spoke.

'Elise? I'm Mr Cuffley. Grace's dad, remember, we met once before.'

She tried to smile.

'I wanted to thank you for looking after Grace,' he was saying. 'I think we owe you a new scarf.' She didn't know what he was talking about but she forced herself to sit up. Jack had disappeared.

'Mr Cuffley,' she said. 'Is Grace OK?'

'She is,' he said. 'And the name's Tim. Do you want to come and see her? She's asking for you.'

He led her through to the ward where Grace was lying in a bed, a bandage covering her right eye. Elise hugged her, then sat to her right side, safely out of her direct vision. 'How are you?' she asked.

'I'm alright,' she said, 'now that they've given me loads of painkillers. I'm not convinced that a black eye is going to be a good look though.'

'Have you spoken to the police, Elise?' asked Mr Cuffley. 'They've questioned Grace already. Not that there was much she could tell them. It's pretty obvious the weather was to blame. I feel sorry for the driver, he must feel terrible, poor chap. In fact, I think I'll go and have a quick word with him. Elise will look after you, won't you Elise?'

She nodded and watched as his long legs disappeared out of the room. Grace tried to sit up, agitated.

'What are you doing?' Elise asked. 'You need to rest!'

Grace's eyes were wild. 'How do we know that was an accident?'

'What do you mean?' Elise wished Mr Cuffley hadn't gone, Grace was clearly still in shock.

'I think we had something to do with the crash. Do you remember what we were doing on the bus?'

Elise screwed up her forehead, trying to pinpoint the exact moment when the bus crashed. She'd been concerned about Grace, pressing her hand on hers, then there was thunder...

'The circles!'

'What?' Grace's lips were pale. An idea was forming in Elise's mind.

'Let me get Jack, I want to tell you both. He's just outside.'

She rushed out of the room. She found Jack in the corridor, spinning an unopened can of coke round and round in his lap.

'Jack!' she said. He jumped up when he saw her, the can clattering to the floor, and pulled her into a hug.

'Sorry I was an ass earlier,' he mumbled. 'It freaks me out when I see you two mind-reading. And given the circumstances...'

She swallowed hard, almost unable to speak at the unexpected proximity of him. 'Forget it,' she said, 'you had a big shock. I need you to come with me.' She released herself slowly, indicating he should follow her as she led the way back to Grace's bed.

'What's so urgent?'

'Remember when I took Grace's hand and pressed it on the bus?' she stroked the circle as she was talking. Jack nodded. 'I could see her circle was itching and mine was too, and I sort of thought if I put them together it might help. The bus crashed straight after. There was a thunder clap, and a huge jolt through my body, but it was a split second before the crash, like electricity, like...'

'Like a lightning strike,' said Jack. 'That's what it sounds like.'

'I felt it too,' Grace said, her eyes huge in her face. 'I knew something wasn't right about it, but . . .'

'I think our touching circles caused it to happen!'

'How can that be?' Jack pulled a face.

'I don't know, but do you understand everything there is to know about lightning and how it affects us?'

Jack sighed. 'No,' he said, 'There is a book somewhere, so rumour has it, but it disappeared centuries ago.'

The three of them sat in silence. The wind was forcing a branch of the tree outside to bash against the window, the rain still coming down hard. Grace was lying down again, staring up at the ceiling.

'There is a way to find out,' Jack said after a while. He held out his hand, palm upwards. Grace stared at him for a moment, then shifted herself up into a sitting position and held her hand out too.

'No!' said Elise.

'Why not?' said Grace. 'My circle is really sensitive, especially to the weather. I want to know what's happening to us. And if Jack's right, nothing will.'

Elise hesitated, then took Jack's hand first, placing her own over the circle. They sat very still. Nothing happened. He grinned and took his hand away. 'There you go.' He pressed his palm against Grace's. Again they waited.

Grace pulled her hand away. 'You think I'm making this up,' she said, pressing her lips together, 'but I know what I felt.'

Jack folded his hands together and Grace held out her hand to Elise, who did the same, carefully pressing the circles together. Grace's hand was icy cold, but sharp hot pinpricks pierced around the circle. She breathed in sharply and raised her eyes to meet Grace's. A tremor ran through Elise's body, then she was in Grace's mind.

`Take Jack's hand!`

Why?

`Just do it!`

Elise reached out for Jack's hand, her eyes still on Grace.

I'm taking his other hand.

A flash shot through three heads

Why?

`You've joined us Jack, haven't you?`

Jack was holding both girls' hands, listening to the conversation that was flowing between their minds.

Yes, I'm here, but our eyes aren't joined. I don't get it.

`We've completed the circle. Both of you close your eyes.`

All three lowered their eyelids simultaneously.

Are you still there?

Yes

Yes

We're connected through the circle now. Count to three and drop hands.

1, 2, 3

Elise opened her eyes first. The others looked dazed, Jack rubbing his eyes with his fist.

'What happened there?' she asked.

'The circles enabled us to have a three way conversation, but only you and Grace were linked by circles. For some reason our circles are more sensitive than Jack's.'

'Or more powerful,' Jack said. 'I've never heard of that before, but The Gift in women is rare – as far as my family is concerned. I'd almost say my dad fears it in a way, but I've never understood why.' His eyes were shining. 'Maybe you have powers that he doesn't know about!'

Mr Cuffley stuck his head around the door. He ran his hands through his hair.

'The driver's being discharged,' he announced. 'God, that's a relief. The roads around here are treacherous, poor bloke. He's pretty shaken up, I can tell you.'

'So there's nothing wrong with him?' Elise asked.

'He's fine, just a few cuts and bruises, a bit shocked, that's all, said the whole thing took him by surprise. He said the rain was coming down so hard, visibility wasn't great. Forget about it now, honey, the doctor's coming in to discharge you in a moment and

I'll take you home. Would you like a lift back, Elise?'

'Yes please,' she said, turning to Jack. 'I know we agreed to talk to Mum, and I do want to, but I don't think tonight's a good idea.'

'I'll ring you tomorrow.' He took her hand, the warmth reassuring her a little. She couldn't wait to get home before the storm came to an end, reassure her mum she was alright and then she had something very urgent to do. She needed to speak to Annie.

CHAPTER 18

Grace was asleep on the back seat by the time Tim pulled up outside the cottage.

'Are you sure she's OK?' Elise asked. Tim nodded.

'She just needs to rest now. She was lucky the glass missed her eye. A couple of inches more and ...' he glanced back at Grace, lines etched onto his face that hadn't been noticeable earlier. 'Hopefully there won't be much of a scar either. The doctor assured me it will fade away with time. She's going to have a pretty impressive shiner on her though.'

Half an hour later she was curled up in her room with a mug of hot chocolate. She thought she'd never escape Mum's fussing. As soon as Mum had gone back downstairs she jumped up and pulled the photograph out from under the bed. Lightning lit up the sky as she blocked out everything apart from the little girl in the photograph. The familiar eyes looked back at hers, then widened. The dark grey became light, almost silver and then she was inside Annie's mind.

You've been gone for ages

So much is happening. The lightning caused an accident today.

Lightning is very powerful. You must be careful. Have you stayed away from the boy?

Jack is my friend, it's complicated. I'm trying to be careful. I met his dad, Mr Warrender

Mr Warrender from the Big House?

Yes, Gorse Hall. He's the ancestor of the Mr Warrender you knew. He's the bad one, not Jack

Jack will be in danger if he crosses his father.

I know. What can I do?

He's looking for something. It's in the cottage. George left it there. You need to find it before he does.

Before who?

Mr Warrender

But what is it? Is it an embroidery?

You found that?

Yes. It says friends forever.

Elise heard Annie gasp, then a choking sound filled her head.

Annie? What is it? Don't cry, please. Did you make it? Annie?

Elise became aware of the rain against the windows, less forceful now, as Annie's face swam back into focus. She stroked her finger over the photograph, her thoughts racing. So Mr

Warrender was looking for something concealed in the cottage, hidden by George many years ago. Not the embroidery, although judging by Annie's reaction she had made that herself. Elise picked up her hot chocolate and drank a mouthful, it was still warm, and she relaxed back against the side of the bed, the noise of the rain now replaced by the sea crashing up and down outside, echoing the thoughts in her head.

There was a light tapping on the door, and Mum's head appeared, framed by the light.

'Are you asleep?'

'No, come in.'

Mum came over and sat down on the end of the bed. She stroked Elise's hair.

'I was so worried when the hospital rang. Thankfully you're alright, but poor Grace. We can get her some flowers tomorrow.'

'Thanks Mum.'

'I had a conversation with Mr Warrender this afternoon.'

Elise pulled herself up onto her elbows, her heartbeat picking up. 'Did he come round?'

'No, he phoned again. He's definitely interested in making me an offer for the cottage.'

'But Mum, I thought you weren't going to sell!'

'Keep calm, darling, I haven't decided anything yet, but he's offering a lot of money.'

'I hope you said no.'

'Elise! I told him I'd think about it. Which I am doing, I wanted to talk to you and consider my options.'

'I don't like him, Mum, Jack . . .'

'Elise, I'm not basing such a huge decision on your likes and dislikes. Whether Jack gets on with his dad or not has no bearing on this.'

'But . . .' – she was properly awake now.

'Look, don't upset yourself. We'll both sleep on it and have a chat in the morning.' She kissed Elise on the forehead and straightened the covers around her, reaching over to turn out the light.

'Alright love? Get some sleep now, eh, you've had a nasty shock. Night love.'

As soon as Elise heard Mum's footsteps descending the creaking stairs she threw back the covers and got out of bed. She switched on her lamp and pulled the diary out from under the mattress. Sleep was the last thing on her mind.

August 1892

I told Mrs Warrender tonight that we were planning to leave town and she did not take the news well. Now I am even more worried about her. Annie was also inconsolable, she tells me she is devoted to George and does not wish to leave him. I explained to her that we are only moving to the next village and she will still be able to see him. She was somewhat reassured by this news; unlike Mrs Warrender who says I am her only friend in the world. I fear this is true for she no longer leaves the house and I suspect that her husband does not allow it.

This morning I received a handwritten note from Mrs Warrender. She says that George is in imminent danger from her husband and wants me to go to her. She speaks of his birthday next month and other strange things. I worry the poor woman is losing her mind.

August 25th

I am concerned for my husband of late, who appears to be changing his mind about moving away. Mr Partington revealed to him that Mr Warrender intends to purchase the land upon which Bramble Cottage is built, and since then Arthur has declared he will never let 'that man' take this cottage away which has been in his family for so long. Worse, he has started to extend the cellar, with the help of his brother, so that we may have an emergency shelter if we need one. I will not oppose his plans, it keeps him occupied and away from the drinking of whisky which he does with increasing frequency, and that does little for his mood. For myself I will be pleased if we do stay, for I have been happy here and my little Annie even more so.

September 20th 1892

I took Annie up to the house today to see George and made the most of the opportunity to see Mrs Warrender. She was up and about, which I took to be a good sign until I realised how feverish her movements were. Her eyes were burning bright, and I almost felt afraid. I asked her if the doctor had visited of late, but she swept away my question with talk of other matters. When I was due to leave, she grabbed my arm very hard, hurting me, and whispered in my ear that her husband would be away on Friday and I had to visit her then, as she had something she wanted me to look after for her.

Elise rested the book on her lap for a moment and gazed out of the window. She could see stars twinkling above through a chink in the curtains. Was this the information she was looking for? She let out the breath she'd been holding in. She shifted position and returned her attention to the diary.

Friday September 23rd

I spent a restless night going over Mrs Warrender's words, rising earlier than usual. I did not mention my worries to Arthur, he has enough to concern himself with at the moment. He left early to speak with Mr Partington. Then as soon as the hour was decent I set off for Gorse Hall.

Mrs Warrender was expecting me, and asked the maid to ensure that we were not disturbed. I hesitate to write down what she told me, as I fear the poor woman is deranged. But tell I must, if only to get the thoughts out of my head, for I may speak to no other of her ramblings.

She sat down opposite me, took hold of my hand in her sparrow like one, and told me a story. I sigh as I write this at how deranged her mind has become. She told me that her husband is an evil man, who has only become so on account of being struck by lightning as a child, which enabled him to read and subvert other people's minds. If this wasn't fanciful enough, she then says that the strike by lightning was pre-arranged, and all males in the family must be struck on the eve of puberty. It is for this reason that she worries about George, as he will be thirteen in a few days time, on the 27th of this month.

I tried to reason with her, to explain that she was ill with a fever, but she was having none of it and became quite distressed. I resolved then to listen to her words, although I do not take them to heart, for I can see how ill she is. She even took me outside the house to point out a field where this ritual is supposedly to take place. It is true, the field behind the house was unnaturally flat with jagged rocks piled up around the edge, but I closed my lips and merely agreed with her. Next she took me back to the house, where she continued her story.

She has found a way, she says, to save George from this ritual. She talked of a Lightning Lore which goes back to ancient times, the whereabouts of which has never been known – the poor woman claims to have found it! She revealed to me a tiny black book full of the smallest writing, all written in capital letters. She did not say how she came about this book; it does indeed look very old and smelt most unpleasant, but she wrapped it in a large white handkerchief and pressed it into my hands. She was shaking, poor woman. She asked me to hide this book in the most secret place I can think of, where it may never be found. That way, her husband may continue to search the house for he knows for certain that it is hidden somewhere in Gorse Hall. And if George were to be put through this terrible

*ordeal, she has the knowledge that there is a way to save him. She has
not read the details, that way her husband may not try and bend her
mind to find out.*

*I took the book from her and promised her I would hide it, it can
do no harm. I am not afraid, for I know she is speaking nonsense. I
have taken advantage of the alterations Arthur has started, to ensure
that indeed it will never be found. Mrs Warrender tells me that if
ever she needs the book, she will find me wherever I am.*

Elise put the diary carefully back in its hiding place and rested
her head on the pillow, eyes wide and looking at the ceiling. One
fact had jumped out at her, and it terrified her. It had taken her
back to a conversation she'd had with Jack about star signs. His
birthday was imprinted in her memory. George was born on the
same day as Jack. She had a very bad feeling about this.

CHAPTER 19

Mum was waiting in the car, the engine running. Elise closed the door behind her and went round to the passenger side. She slung her bag onto the back seat and settled into the front.

'Ready?' Mum said, holding out the seatbelt. Elise took a deep breath, then let it out slowly.

'Let me do it,' she said, avoiding looking at her mum. She flinched as the slipperiness of the belt registered in her mind, but she secured the lock and went straight for the radio to drown out the noise in her head. Mum put the car into gear and they headed off into town.

Mum went off to park the car, while Elise went into the florists to buy some flowers. She picked out a bright bouquet of oranges and yellows, she was sure Grace would like those. They walked through the park to Grace's house. She remembered the phone call Mum had taken earlier.

'Who was it that rang this morning Mum?' asked Elise.

'Mr Warrender.'

'What did you tell him?'

'Nothing so far. I haven't decided anything yet, I need to speak to my solicitor first. It's not an easy decision to make. Mr Warrender is coming round on Friday afternoon, and that's when I'll give him my decision.'

Elsie scowled at the floor.

'Don't look like that Elise, we've already talked about this.'

'I don't trust him Mum.'

'Now you're being silly.'

They walked in silence for the rest of the way. Elise focused her attention away from Mum and counted the cracks in the paving stones instead.

Mr Cuffley looked thrilled to see them.

'Come in!' he said. 'Grace is still in bed, but you can pop up and see her if you like, while your mum and I have a cup of coffee. Is that alright with you, Mrs Martin?'

'Sarah, please.'

'Tim. Let me put these flowers in water and you can take them up to Grace.' He took a glass down from a shelf and filled it with water.

'Take those sunglasses off Elise,' Mum hissed, 'you look ridiculous.'

Elise took the shades off but put them back on as son as she had left the adults in the kitchen. She followed the sound of music which was coming from Grace's room.

'Come in,' Grace yelled.

Grace squealed when she saw the flowers.

Grace's room was covered in posters, and her dressing table was littered with make up, pots of nail varnish, lipsticks and tiny bottles of perfume which covered the surface entirely. Clothes were strewn all over the floor.

'Excuse the mess,' Grace said, 'it's always like this. Come and sit up here.' She patted the bed and moved her legs out of the way. She was still in her pyjamas, but sitting on top of the bed. 'Put the flowers on the dressing table. They're gorgeous, thanks.'

Elise pushed aside a heap of eye shadows and lipsticks to make a space for the flowers amongst the make up.

'Mum's downstairs, having coffee with your dad.'

'Great,' said Grace, 'he never has anyone round. It will do him good and hopefully stop him fussing over me for a bit.'

'How's your eye?' asked Elise. Grace's left eye was covered in a dressing.

'Still a bit sore, but I can take this off tomorrow. I've promised dad I'll stay in today but I'm bored already. Has anything happened? Have you heard from Jack?'

'No, I'm going to ring him this afternoon,' She told Grace what she had found out in the diary. Grace became extremely animated at the mention of the book.

'Do you think this is the mysterious hidden thing? It must be – and both Mr Warrender and Mary are looking for it. We have to find out where it is and get to it before he does. You can't let your mum sell the cottage, you can't.'

'Calm down,' Elise said, 'I've been thinking about this all night. There might be something more about it in the diary or with the rest of the stuff. I'm going into town after this, to the library. I'm going to see if I can find out anything more about lightning, maybe even ask the librarian if it's possible to speak to her grandmother.'

'Didn't you say she wouldn't talk about it?'

Elise shrugged. 'I'm going to try. I can't think what else to do.'

'I wish I could come with you.'

'You have to rest – you do look tired.'

'A lot of it is the mind reading, it knocks me out. Doesn't it you?"

Elise nodded.

Grace flopped back on the bed. 'Yeah, it does. But I'm coming over to yours tomorrow. I'll get Dad to drop me when he goes to work. Then we can do a proper search. When's Mr Warrender coming round again?'

'Friday.'

'So there isn't much time. You'd better get down to thelibrary. And you know what this means, don't you?'

'What?'

'No way can Mr Warrender find out what we know. We have to keep away from him, we can't risk him discovering our secrets.'

As Elise strolled into town later, she decided to try and see if she could find anything out about George too, maybe look at the newspapers again. She hadn't told Grace her fears about the coincidence of Jack's birthday, it was probably her imagination going wild again.

The library counter appeared empty at first until she caught sight of Sheila in the little office tucked away behind the desk, eating a biscuit. She came out when she saw Elise.

'Hello, love. You caught me out – having a quick tea break. You'll have to tell me your name again.'

'Elise.'

'That's a pretty name. More research is it today?'

She nodded. 'I've found a diary in the house, and there are some names I want to look up.'

'A diary? That's interesting. What's the date?'

'1892 I think.'

'Gosh, that's fascinating.' She walked over to one of the large round tables in the library and sat down. Elise followed her. 'I'd love to have a look at it some day.'

'Maybe,' said Elise.

Sheila laughed. 'I know, you want to discover all the secrets first, that's perfectly understandable. I bet my grandmother would love to see it.' She frowned. 'She's very funny about the past. I wish she'd open up more, because, well, she's old and sadly she won't be around forever and her knowledge will go to heaven with her unless I can get her to talk about it. I'll tell her about the diary, see how she reacts to that. Whose diary is it?'

'Mary, her name is. Mary Darley. And the person I want to find out about is called George, George Warrender. Actually, anything about the Warrenders would be useful.'

'The Warrenders? You mean the family from Gorse Hall?'

She nodded.

Sheila took off her glasses and polished them on her shirt. 'Let me think. You can try the newspapers again of course, I'll set you up with those and I'll go and see if I can find any books that might help.'

Elise spent the rest of the morning ploughing through the old newspapers. There were many references to Mr Warrender in relation to his business and his land, but no news items relating to George. Sheila came over with a couple of books, so once Elise had finished with the newspapers she turned to the books. One of them was a very large volume which she hadn't seen before. '*History of streets in Eldon,*' it was called.

Elise turned to the index for G and found the page reference for Gorse Hall. She read through the two page listing. The only piece of useful information was the date of Mr Warrender's death and that he was succeeded by his younger son, Thomas. There was no mention of George. What had happened to George and why hadn't he inherited the estate? Solving this mystery was clearly linked to what Annie wanted her to find out.

She stretched and checked the time on her phone. A text had come in from Jack.

What are you up to?

She tapped out a reply.
Library – Warrender research!

Anything interesting you want to share?

A little. Grace is coming over tomorrow, want to join us?

I can make it after lunch, how's that?

Cool! See you then

She was smiling as she put her phone away in her bag and piled the books up. Surely Grace and Jack would become friends eventually. She took them over to the library desk. Sheila was stamping some books for another customer so she waited until she'd finished.

'Any luck?' the librarian asked.

'A bit, I think. Can I photocopy this?'

'Of course, the photocopier is over there. It's ten pence a sheet.'

Elise took the book over to the photocopier and scanned the sheets in.

'There is one more thing,' she said, as she put the book back on the counter, and counted out thirty pence for Sheila. 'Have you ever heard anything about a Lightning Lore?'

Sheila opened her eyes wide. 'A Lightning Lore, whatever's that?'

'Oh it's just something I read about in the old papers at home.'

'Well I can ask Gran when I get home but I don't hold out much hope. Do you want to give me your mobile number, then if I do find anything out I can let you know to come in again?'

'Great, thanks,' Elise said, writing her number down on a piece of scrap paper. Sheila folded it and put it in her pocket.

Elise spent the evening going back through the papers in the box. She couldn't find any more references to George, and there was no mention of Thomas at all. She read through the excerpt she'd photocopied so many times she almost knew it by heart. After a couple of hours she gave up and went downstairs spent to watch TV with Mum.

'I can't believe it's raining again,' Mum said, as she drew the curtains in the living room. 'I've never known such bad weather. I really don't know whether I could stand to live here with this constant rain. It's supposed to be summer, for heaven's sake!'

Elise felt her stomach clenching.

Does that mean you've changed your mind about staying?'

Mum looked over at Elise. 'You like it here, don't you?'

Elise nodded. 'I've made friends, Mum. You don't know what that's like.'

Mum sat down next to her and ruffled her hair. 'Oh, I think I do. I'm pleased for you. They both seem really nice. Grace's dad is a very charming man.'

'Oh no Mum you don't fancy him do you?'

Mum burst out laughing. 'Don't be silly. But seriously, I won't do anything drastic. I've got an appointment with the solicitor tomorrow, and Mr Warrender is coming over on Friday. You really don't need to worry – I want what's best for both of us.'

They settled down to watch a film, but after only fifteen minutes the screen flickered and the picture disappeared. Moments later there was a clattering sound on the roof. Mum got up to look out of the window.

She sighed. 'That's all we need. I think the wind has knocked the aerial off the roof. Are you really sure you like living out in the sticks? We might as well go to bed. I'll have to sort this out in the morning.'

Hours later an electric flash lit up the room and Elise sat up in bed, her pulse racing. The cottage was being pounded from all sides by wind and rain and the window lit up every few seconds with flashes of lightning. The window frame rattled incessantly and Elise feared her heart was about to burst through her throat. She went to the window and jumped back as once more the garden was illuminated.

She couldn't stop worrying about Jack. Each flash of lightning caused her nerves to jangle. The hairs on her arm were standing on end and she couldn't keep still. There was no way she could block out the lightning, so she swung her legs out of bed and reached for the photograph. With shaking hands she took the envelope from her dressing table and pulled it out, before sitting down cross-legged on the floor. Then she spread the familiar face out on her lap and focused her eyes on Annie. The grey irises opened up to her, relieved.

You came!

I need your help. Jack is in danger

I warned you of this when we last spoke

I know but we are running out of time. His father is trying to persuade us to sell the house to him. Why does he want it?

There is something that he must find

I don't know where to look. Can't you help me?

I can only tell you what I know. After that you will be on your own. I know nothing of the hiding place. Please find it Elise. You are the only one who can set me free or...

Or what?

Or I will never be able to rest in peace. Listen carefully now, for I am about to tell you my story.

CHAPTER 20

ANNIE

M other had tried to stop me from going out; the storm was bad the night before, branches of the tree had come down and she was frightened. It took me a while to convince her that it was over and I had survived; imagine! I was struck by lightning and escaped with nothing but a burn on my hand. At last I was on my way, almost running along the cliff top, so eager was I to see George.

'I hope he likes his present,' that's what I was thinking as I willed my feet to go faster, cursing my skirts as I tried to hold the folds out of the muddy soil. It was George's thirteenth birthday and I had been making his present all year. It was a piece of embroidery, sewn by hand and I'd spent hours every evening, peering at the material by candlelight. But it was worth it, for George. I loved him you see, Elise, I'd always loved him and he loved me too. My earliest memory was playing hide and seek with George up at the Big House, while mum swept and polished. I helped her of course, but there were lots of times when she would sit with Mrs Warrender when the master was out on business and George and I had the run of the house. I was nervous too though, for once he had seen the embroidery there would be no going back, when he read the words I had lovingly embroidered for him.

'Forever friends,' it said, with tiny daisies entwined with the letters.

'You can't write that Annie!' Mum had scolded me, but I threw my arms around her neck and covered her in kisses and tickles until she begged me to stop. She thinks it's just childish nonsense but George will know I am serious.

When I arrived at the Big House I went around the back and into the kitchen, where the warm smells made me instantly hungry. Martha sent Betty the housemaid to tell George I was here, but then she told me to sit down and I could tell by her eyes that something was wrong.

'What is it Martha?' I asked. 'Is it George? What's happened?'

'Master George is not harmed,' she said and I let out the breath which I had been holding as I awaited her answer, but her next words made me swallow it down again. 'But he may not want to see you this morning.'

'Why not? It's his birthday.' She shook her head and suddenly I was afraid.

'Is it Mr Warrender?' I whispered, scared to voice my fears out loud.

'No child,' she shook her head but her eyes were dark.

A soup bubbled on the stove and as my eyes focused on the flame a noise from behind made me turn around. Betty had returned.

'I'm sorry, he can't see you today,' she said, her eyes avoiding mine.

'Why not?' I gasped, willing my pumping chest to be still.

'I don't know,' she said, 'everything is topsy turvy today.' As she spoke these words it was only then that I realized that she was not wearing her usual sunny disposition. 'What is it, Betty? What's happened?'

Betty was much younger than Martha and I knew she cared for me; she often teased me for being sweet on George when Martha wasn't there to scold her. She crossed over to me and took my small hands in hers. 'You should go home,' she said, 'the family have business to attend to and they won't want you here.'

'But it's George's birthday, I brought his present. Please Betty, I have to see him.'

She looked around and then took my arm and pulled me outside to the shelter of the porch behind the back door.

'What is it Betty, what's wrong with George? I have to know.' I could see indecision crossing her face. Glancing around to check that we were alone she nodded.

'I know how fond you are of George, but you did not hear this from my lips. Last night George went through the Lightning.'

'Lightning? What do you mean? I know there was a storm last night… I was struck, look.' I held out my hand. Her eyes were dark as she took in the curiously circular mark on my hand. I distracted her from it, impatient now. 'But tell me about George.'

She sank down on the ledge and motioned for me to sit next to her. She was silent for a while before she started speaking. 'The Warrender family go back many generations and a curious power exists within the family, which enables the male of the species to be able to read minds. In order to acquire this gift, as they call it, the male has to be struck by lightning close to the eve of his thirteenth birthday. Special conditions have been created within the grounds of Gorse House which enable this to happen. George is thirteen today, as you know, and last night he went through the ritual. He did not want it to happen, which is unusual, but his father was adamant. He is of the age at which the ability to utilise the power is at its strongest.'

'Why did George not want this to happen? Wouldn't it be amazing to read other people's minds?'

Betty shook her head, her expression sad. 'George is a good child, and even though he is so young, I think he realizes what will happen to him.'

'What do you mean?'

She sighed. 'Initially the Gift was used for good, but for generations now the Warrenders have used the Gift to manipulate people to do *their will. Why do you think they own so much land? Over the years they have persuaded small farm holders to go into business with them, only to be ruined shortly after.' She lowered her voice. 'Mr Warrender is by far the worst, he will force George to continue his evil work.'*

'How do you know about this? Did Martha tell you?'

She shook her head. 'My grandmother worked for the family, and my mother before me. I would rather work anywhere but here, but I have no choice. Where else is there to work after all?' She was right; the Warrenders were the only employers in the area. They owned all the nearby property and businesses, and Mr Warrender was the most powerful man on the parish council. 'Grandmother warned me about the family history; her father lost everything to old Mr Warrender and the family never recovered.' Betty looked at me directly, her eyes glinting. 'But I intend to get away from here, to better myself. I will not let the Warrenders destroy my family.'

My head was reeling and my body started to shake.

'There is nothing you can do, child.' She placed her warm hand on my cold one.

'But George? I don't want him to change!'

'There is no known way to reverse the process. Rumour exists that there is a way, but it is not known to the family.'

'Your grandmother! She may know.'

Betty cast her eyes down. 'Grandmother is very old, even if she does know anything it will not help us now.'

'You have to be wrong! I won't let this happen to George. I'm going to tell my parents, I'll tell anyone who will listen.' My voice had risen now. Betty got to her feet.

'No! You must not speak of this to a soul. Come, you're shivering, let's go inside.' She motioned me towards the door but stopped just outside. 'Now go into the kitchen and let's get you warm.' She pushed me forwards and I stepped through the open door. And came face to face with Mr Warrender.

The master of the house was breathing deeply, his face a dark shade of crimson. Immediately I looked away, anxious lest my face give away my terror. Had he heard me? I wished that I were back at home, mother would know what to do. Betty looked petrified.

'Haven't you got a job to do?' he barked, and she bobbed into a curtsey and scurried out of the room, shooting an apologetic glance at me as she went. His large figure blocked the door and as if reading my mind he reached behind him and slammed it shut. Terror rose in my throat and I was unable to prevent a small whimpering sound from escaping.

'What are you doing down here?'

'I..I came to see George.' My hands clutched at my bag; I could feel the embroidery safe inside it, which comforted me a little.

'George isn't in the kitchen, is he? What were you bothering my kitchen staff about?'

'Nothing,' I said, 'I'm sorry; I didn't mean to distract Betty from her work.

His eyes narrowed and he took a step towards me when the door opened and Martha came in. My heart leapt straight into my throat and pounded loudly in my ears.

'Whatever are you doing here child?' she asked. She grabbed me by the arm and dragged me towards the door. 'I'm so sorry Sir, she shouldn't be down here. I've given Betty a piece of my mind and she's hard at work now. She's a good girl really, just easily distracted. Annie came to see Master George on account of it being his birthday, she didn't mean any harm.' She ushered me out of the room and I hurried through the kitchen, anxious to get away from Mr Warrender. Moments later the back door slammed and we both watched through the window as he crossed the yard.

'You silly girl!' Martha said, 'Betty told me all this nonsense she's been telling you. You're to forget you ever heard any of it. She gets these fancy ideas in her head and she doesn't know what she's talking

about half the time.'

'But George, the lightning...'

'Hush!' she said and I could see fear in her eyes. I shivered.

'I want to see George,' I said. 'I've still got his present in my bag. I'll be quick, I promise.'

Her eyes travelled to the window where Mr Warrender was by now a distant blob on the horizon. 'Very well,' she said, 'but hurry now, then you get off home. Master George is tired today.'

I was already on my way out as I called my thanks to her and left her still gazing out of the window. I took the stairs two at a time and knocked loudly on the playroom door. I heard a noise so I pushed the door open, he was sitting on a couch by the window, a book face down on the floor next to him.

'Oh,' I said, 'May I come in?'

He looked across at me and I noticed that his eyes had a strange glow about them. He swung his legs down onto the floor and pulled his broken glasses on.

'George,' I said, crossing the room and kneeling down on the floor. 'What's happened? I've brought you your birthday present.'

He rubbed his forehead as if trying to erase a pain. 'Strange things have been happening,' he said. 'I want to tell you, but I'm scared for you.' He reached for his spectacles, but the left lens was cracked and crudely held together by tape. There were marks on his face, as if he'd been scratched. He bit down hard on his lip and I could see the colour ebb and flow from it. 'What happened to your spectacles?' I asked. 'Look at me, George.'

'I can't,' he said. 'My eyes are sore.' He paused for a moment, then took off his spectacles and raised his eyes briefly to me. A strange light shone out of them and he quickly replaced the lenses.

'George,' I pleaded, his present forgotten now.

'I can't!' His voice was harsh as he repeated the words and I flinched, my turn now to press my lips together to stop the tears from

flowing out of my eyes. 'You'll be in danger if I tell,' he added, his tone kinder. 'Please Annie, listen to me for once. You have to go away from here, I can't see you any more.'

'I know what it is and I'm not frightened,' I uttered one truth, 'Betty told me about the lightning.'

His eyes widened and he almost jumped off the bed. 'Betty? What did she tell you?'

I repeated what she had told me earlier. He sat back down again to listen but his face paled the more I spoke. He avoided my eyes and I began to regret speaking.

'Is she right George, did this happen to you?'

He nodded slowly and then words tumbled out of his mouth.

'Everything she said is correct. My father made me undergo the Lightning last night, I tried to resist, but this is what happens when anyone tries to resist my father.' He stroked the broken frame of his spectacles and I gasped. 'He pushed me to the ground and tried to stand on them. He knows how little I am able to see without them. I knew then there was no point in struggling further. I gave in and let him do it, but I won't become like him, I won't.' His face was all screwed up and I knew he was fighting back tears. 'I tried so hard to get away yesterday, there were only five hours to go. I was so close.'

'Five hours?'

'Until midnight. Then it would have been too late. But I was struck at seven o'clock, you must have heard the storm?'

'Heard it? But I was struck too! Not deliberately of course. Look!' I held out my hand, the perfect circle still etched into my skin. George grabbed my hand and let out a cry. 'What's this?'

'It's where the lightning struck me. I was down by the woods at the back of our house. At first the flash hurt my eyes, then afterwards I was left with this mark and my hand was throbbing all night.'

'So you got this at seven o'clock too? Are you sure? Was it the first bolt that came down?'

'Yes,' I nodded. 'It was very close. What's the matter?'

He closed his eyes for a moment and when he spoke his words travelled slowly.

'I have this mark too. Look at my hand.' He raised his palm to reveal the very same dark circle.

'I don't understand,' I said, raising my eyes to meet his. As I raised my eyes he removed his spectacles and looked straight back at me. The blue glow was clear now and a flash pierced through my head. Then I felt as if I was falling, Elise, falling into George's mind. I saw everything that had happened last night, I saw his pain and I also saw his love for me. And I spoke to him then, without words and I told him about the present I had spent so many long hours making and what it meant and how I would always fight for him. That's when he told me how the first person one speaks to after the Lightning influences the persons behaviour forever. And how glad he was that it was me, but how very afraid. For his father was meant to be that person and there was nothing he could do now. Unless I were to die which would reverse the process…

Pain was shooting through my eyes and I was dragged out of George's mind as suddenly as I'd fallen in. Large hands gripped my shoulders and I tried feebly to shake them off, but my mind was still dazed and my body wouldn't respond. The first thing I was aware of was a smell of burning, no, it was tobacco, then George's face came into focus. His mouth was open in anguish and he was struggling to his feet and everything speeded up, faster and faster as he lunged towards me and started shouting.

'Get off her! Get off her!'

I could tell by his face that it was his father who was gripping my shoulders and in my panic I struck backwards with my elbow, pointed and hard. It landed on the large mound of his stomach and there was a wheezing gasp and his grip loosened. George pushed him and I was free.

'Run!' he yelled, 'Run Annie!'

I hesitated for a second, reluctant to leave him, but he shouted again and the crack in his voice propelled me on. I charged out through the door, my breath shooting out in terrified gasps. I left the house by the side door and hared over the fields, terror guiding me. My feet slid in the wet mud more than once and I glanced back as often as I dared; terrified of what I might see, hoping at the same time that George would be behind me. The events of the last hour were so out of this world that I half believed I might be in a dream. Tears were pouring down my face by the time I arrived at the cottage, and I ran around to the back door and shoved hard against it. The house was silent, but my breathing was loud, gasps and cries escaping from my mouth as I regained my senses. Then I ran from room to room, hoping that mother or father were sitting quietly out of sight, but alas the house was indeed empty.

Regaining my senses, I realized that Mr Warrender would come after me and I ran once again around the house, barring the doors and windows. I lit the large wax candle on the mantlepiece as the first hint of darkness was in the skies and it would soon be inky black both inside and out. I was shaking now, awareness of what had happened between myself and George hitting me with full force. We had entered each other's thoughts and he loved me. We were going to be together after all. He still hadn't seen the gift I had crafted which was languishing in my pouch on his bedroom floor, if his father hadn't destroyed it by now. If he hadn't destroyed George . . . a sob escaped from my throat again and I crossed to the window to look out across the field. The wind was whipping the trees up into a frenzy and the long grass swayed to and fro, as if angry. As the sky appeared to darken before me a fear crept over my body, and at the same time a tiny figure appeared on the horizon, making it's way towards the cottage. I prayed it would be George and as he grew within my vision I thanked God that my prayers were answered. Still in his shirt sleeves he ran blindly across the grass; my heart lurched as he lost his footing once, twice, then as he came properly within my vision I could see that he was clutching his spectacles in his hand. I pulled hard on the front door, which was stiff with little use as we always went out through the back way.

'George!' I shouted, 'over here!' and he ran towards me; I could see now that his father was pursuing him across the field. 'Quick!' I grabbed his arm and pulled him through the heavy door, then pushed against it with all my weight. I pulled the lock into place and we faced each other, both panting; George from exertion of his weak chest and me from panic. Yet I was happy to see him, for awful pictures had been playing through my mind of what fate would befall him, left in his father's clutches.

'You have to get away,' he gasped, 'he'll be here in a moment. He saw the lightning mark on your hand and he knows now, there's no telling what he might do to you.'

'But how can I? I won't leave you alone with him.' Our eyes locked and the pain made me shudder at first but then I could see his thoughts.

You must leave without him seeing you. But how can you? All exits are visible

There is one. My father has been excavating under the house. He suspects there is valuable rock deep among the foundations. There is an exit at the far end, which leads into the field at the back of our garden.

There is something I must tell you. There is an ancient document in existence, containing what is known as the lightning lore.

How do you know of this?

Betty brought me word from her grandmother. She believes it was given to your mother for safekeeping.

Mother?

Enough of this, we waste precious time. He will be here soon. You must get far away, you'll have to leave the village, get as many miles from here as you can.

I can't leave my mother – if what you say is true then she may be in danger.

You have to; I don't think you understand how ruthless my father is.

I'm scared, I've never been anywhere alone before

You won't be alone. I'm coming with you. But if anything should happen to me you must retrieve the Lore

Why?

Because the Lightning Lore contains the key to our freedom. With that document we will be able to free ourselves

A banging and hollering at the front door broke into our consciousness and forced our eyes to unlock. His thoughts swirled away from me and the horror of the present swooped down into place. A terrible crashing sound filled my head as something pounded against the front door, then over and over the same noise, accompanied by the creaks and groans of wood splitting.

'He's got an axe!' shouted George. He was holding his spectacles *against his head, but it did not hide the determined look in his eyes.*

'The passage,' I whispered, 'it's our only chance.' I took his hand and we ran through to the kitchen, my heart lurching inside my chest as I heard the sound of the wooden door falling in. There was a roar as Mr Warrender burst into the house, his heavy footsteps making the floor shudder.

'Where is she?' he bellowed. George had reached the larder and I pointed out the door, which was hidden behind a large sack of flour. He crouched beside it, fiddling with some kind of a catch, then pushed forwards. I glanced over my shoulder to see Mr Warrender coming into the room. George disappeared into the open space and beckoned to me to follow.

'Stop!' Mr Warrender was closer now, his bulk slowing him down and causing him to stop and gather together his breath. As I started to lower myself into the passageway, his eyes bulged and with an almighty yell he grabbed the candleholder from the mantelpiece and hurled it towards me. I heard a thud as it hit my head and then I was falling down to the floor. I searched for George's face as a searing warmth spread across my back and a smell and a crackling sound arose as flames spread through my dress and lit up my hair as my screams filled the air. My head was thick, dull, my limbs unable to move. George's eyes were dull, but his thoughts were clear.

Fire, no, Annie, what has he done?

You have to get away George, run, run for me.

Annie? Annie, speak to me, where are you Annie, don't leave me

Flames swept across my face and I could no longer see or feel and thick black smoke filled my lungs and my mind. As I departed, I tried to find him, to speak to him one last time.

I will never leave you George, until I have my revenge.

That was how I died, Elise, and I have been waiting all these years for someone to release me.

But how can I do that?

I believe the passage still exists. I need you to retrieve the Lightning Lore and find out what happened to George. That is how you will free me from the photograph, and let me rest in peace.

CHAPTER 21

The wind tugged at the side gate as Elise pushed against it, almost falling out into the alleyway. Leaves swirled around her feet as she secured the gate. The sound of a bicycle caused her to look up.

'Morning!' The postman swung his leg over the saddle and leant the bike against a tree. 'You're up early.'

She nodded. 'Early morning walk. Are there any letters for us?'

'Just one,' he said, 'for a Ms Sarah Martin. Is that you?'

She smiled. 'No, that's my mum.' She took it from him and posted it through the letter box.

'Enjoy your walk!' he said, 'mind you don't go too close to the cliff edge, it's a bit blowy out there this morning.'

He whistled loudly as he cycled off down the path, waving as he went. Elise was glad of the wind blowing in her face, waking her up. She couldn't shift the wedge of sadness which had lodged deep inside her after reading of Annie's fate. Seeing the newspaper report had been bad enough, but hearing Annie's account had sliced her in two. Tears had spilled out of her eyes and she'd longed to share her story with someone. She daren't tell Mum, she would blame her OCD again, she'd hinted before now that Elise's obsessive thoughts were her biggest worry. And the counting had been getting less, she'd really been making an effort not to do it as much.

She wished she could talk to Jack. He hadn't phoned yesterday, despite his promises. She took her phone out of her pocket to check it. Still nothing. Her stomach lurched as she imagined him at home with his father, those eyes following him around. How would they know if he'd got to him? She wanted to believe that he would be strong enough to withstand him, but …

The path turned as she followed the cliff along. She could see the sea now, the wind picking up the waves and throwing them through the air. Dark grey clouds puffed along overhead, threatening to swell and burst. Ever since arriving in Eldon the weather appeared to worsen, the further she delved into the past. A large gnarled tree trunk lay on the grass, and she sat down on it, watching the sea. Jack's face drifted into her mind again and she took out her phone and typed out a message.

Are you coming over later?

A reply arrived almost instantly.

Sure. Is Grace still coming?

Yes. Is that a problem?

Be careful what you say to her.

Why?

I'll explain later.

Elise threw the phone down on the grass. Why was he being so difficult about Grace? Elise had seen inside Grace's mind, she trusted her. She kicked her feet against the tree trunk, irritation bubbling up inside her. She wasn't going to lose the first friend she'd made in ages.

A man was walking along the sea front now, a little shaggy dog running along ahead of him, his short legs speeding through the water, splashes flying up around him. Watching the sea calmed her, and tears sprung into her eyes with unexpected force. She loved it here, she couldn't go back to London, but how was she going to persuade Mum not to sell? Why did Mr Warrender have to exist? Her pulse was quickening again, the beats pounding in her throat, and she closed her eyes and counted down from one hundred.

A beep from her phone made her open her eyes, and she reached down to pick it up from the floor. It was a text from an unknown number. She opened the message, curious to see who it was from.

Hello Elise it's Sheila from the library. I asked Gran about the Warrenders and the Lightning Lore and she asked me to pass on a message. She wants you to forget all about it and keep away from Mr Warrender. She insisted I send you this. It all sounds very dramatic to me!

Elise texted back a non-committal thank you and set off on the path back home, her mind spinning. Sheila couldn't possibly understand, but the old lady must know what all this was about. She couldn't wait for Grace to come round. Mr Warrender was due tomorrow – if they could find what he was looking for before he did, then he wouldn't be interested in the cottage any more. Spurred on by this realization she walked as fast as she could back to the cottage.

Elise was buzzing by the time Grace arrived later that morning. Her cheek was bruised and dark glasses covered her eyes.

'I've got an excuse for wearing these now,' she said, waving to her dad as he drove off, his exhaust pipe spewing out clouds of dark smoke.

'Dad's being so attentive, it's doing my head in. He wants me to stay here tonight, is that OK? He's got to work this evening and doesn't want to leave me alone.'

'That's good,' said Elise. 'It gives us plenty of time. Mum's gone into town,' she explained, 'so we can talk freely. I need your help to find something and we have to do it while they are all out. How are you feeling?'

'Much better. I slept for so long. You don't look like you've slept at all!'

'I haven't,' she said. 'I'll tell you why in a minute.'

'Have you heard from Jack?'

'Yes. He's coming over later. I haven't told you what happened at the library. I found out that George had a younger brother, who inherited everything.'

'Mary said Mrs Warrender was pregnant in the diary, didn't she? So that must have been the brother. What was his name?'

'Thomas.'

'So George must have died before he did, but we don't know when.'

'No, but there's loads more to tell you. I think I know what we might be looking for.'

They sat down at the kitchen table and she told Grace everything that had happened the night before and why they needed to search the kitchen.

'I think we're right not to tell Jack about this. Living with his dad makes him vulnerable. It's the right decision, Elise.'

'I know. I can't help thinking about the fire and what the old Mr Warrender was capable of. Annie knew she was about to die, and she's stuck not knowing what happened to George. It's awful.'

'Stop it, you're not to think like that.'

Elise glanced at the large clock on the wall and jumped to her feet. 'Come on! We need to get on with finding this passage before Mum gets back. It has to be behind one of these cupboards. Are you sure you're up to it?'

'Stop fussing. You sound like Dad.'

Grace set about clearing the old pantry. It was a large stone cupboard in the corner and was crammed full of food stuffs that looked as if they had been there for years.

'Do you think your aunt was some kind of hoarder?' asked Grace. 'I've never seen so much stuff. I'm going to have to take everything out to get to the back.'

'Mum will be pleased. She's been moaning about all this stuff ever since we got here.'

By the time Grace had reached the tins of beans which were piled up at the back of the pantry she was sweating. 'This is exhausting,' she said, 'but I think I can see something that could be a door.'

'Let me take over for a bit,' said Elise. 'You probably shouldn't be doing this. It was only yesterday that you were in hospital – I don't want you passing out on me!'

Grace crawled backwards out of the cupboards and sat down at the table. Her skin was pale.

'Just sit there for a moment.' Elise crouched down to peer into the pantry. 'Hey, you're right! I reckon if I move the rest of these cans we'll be able to get to it.'

Grace sank into the chair. Elise disappeared inside the pantry and started shifting the cans.

'Yes!' Elise yelled, and crawled back out of the cupboard. 'Bring me the torch! It's by the back door.' Grace went to the back door and grabbed the torch and rushed to peer over her shoulder.

'Look!' Elise directed the beam to the back of the cupboard. Her hands were filthy.

'What is it?' Grace's voice was loud, filling up the small space.
'There!'

It was the outline of a door, with a rusty lock bolted across the middle. 'I think we've found what we were looking for!'

The shrill sound of the telephone ringing in the hall outside made them both start. They scrambled out of the cupboard and Elise went to answer it. She came back into the room, frowning.

'What's the matter?' asked Grace.

'That was Jack. He sounded really strange.' He hadn't answered any of her questions. He wanted to know what we'd been doing.'

'What did you say?' Grace realised she was holding her breath.

Elise was pulling on her lip. 'I didn't tell him anything.'

'Good.'

'Is it?' Elise sighed. 'This is so hard. I'm stuck in the middle of you two, and I don't know who to believe.'

'You trust me, don't you? You've read my mind after all.'

'Yes, I do, but Jack doesn't, and he can be very convincing. He's worried that his dad had got some kind of hold of you – which you may not even know about. But then, when he sounds different, like he did then, I worry that he's let Mr Warrender mind bend him. He had the opportunity last night after all. How are we to know his dad hasn't influenced him?

'You're right, it's difficult for you,' Grace said, 'but I'm glad you didn't tell him about that.' She nodded towards the cupboard, the open door waiting for them.

It only took a few minutes to completely clear the panel at the back of the cupboard. Once they had moved the last of the dusty cans out of the way, they both sat back on their knees and stared at it.

'I'm scared now,' Elise admitted.

'Remind me what Annie said again.'

'She said that it's a small chamber which leads out into the back of the garden. George reckoned something was hidden down there.' She bashed herself on the head in an exaggerated fashion. 'This has to be what Mr Warrender is after doesn't it?'

'Of course.' Grace's eyes were shining. 'We'd better get on with looking then.'

Elise remained still.

'What's the matter?'

'What if George never got out of the passage? He might have been trapped, and…' Her hands flew to her mouth. 'Oh no, I don't know if I can go in there.'

'We have to. We're doing it to help Jack, remember. I'll go first.'

She pulled on the handle and tugged hard, falling back against Elise as the door flew open. They both stared for a moment and then burst out laughing.

'It's pitch black in there. Pass me the torch,'

Elise passed the torch to Grace. Grace pointed the beam into the dark hole and wrinkled her nose.

'Here goes,' she said, and climbed into the darkness.

CHAPTER 22

The room was large but very cold. Elise shivered as she took in the pile of rotting old cushions on the floor. Other than that it appeared to be empty. She pulled her sleeves down over her hand and buried them deep into her pockets. If she didn't touch anything then maybe she could control the panic. She didn't want Grace to realise how scared she was, but Grace's attention was on the cushions, she was poking at them with her foot, sending clouds of dust into the air. She wrinkled her nose in disgust.

'It stinks down here.'

Grace went to the far end of the room where a slither of light could be seen at floor level. 'Here's the hole which leads out into the garden.' She shivered, clasping her arms around herself. 'There's a terrible draught coming in. I wonder whereabouts it comes out in the garden.' Elise came and looked over her shoulder.

'What are you waiting for then? Get down into that hole!'

Elise made sure her skin was completely covered, before reluctantly lowering herself into the hole, and crawling through a passage which smelled of damp and eggs. As she straightened herself up to standing the wind blew her backwards and she steadied herself as she emerged into the open air. The fresh air took her by surprise. Tall trees surrounded her, and as she turned around to get her bearings, her eyes took in the very flat grass, rocks piled neatly around the edges. She was at the back of the wood. Grace scrambled up out of the passage behind her, her hair blowing all over her face.

'This is where I got struck by lightning,' said Elise. 'The day after we arrived here.' She shivered.

Grace was staring at the field. 'This is exactly how the field looked at Gorse Hall, when I saw it in Mr Warrender's thoughts, I mean. It's kind of weirdly flattened, can you see?'

Elise nodded, looking around at the rectangular space in front of the trees. The grass around it was wilder, uncared for.

'Let's go back inside,' Grace said, 'it's freezing. We don't want anyone to find us down here.'

She led the way back up through the garden to the kitchen, rubbing the mud off her clothes. The house was still empty. It was three o'clock.

'I need to start looking for the document.'

'Do you reckon it will still be there?'

Elise shrugged. 'Listen out for the car and shout if you want me to come back out, OK?'

Elise stood in front of the dark entrance. To search properly she would need to feel around among the bricks, the thought of which made her feel as if tiny creatures were crawling around inside her skin. She started to count her heartbeats.

'Elise!'

'I'm going,' she said, forcing herself to stop counting and take a step forward, not wanting Grace to know what was preventing her from going back inside. She closed her eyes and thought about George, and Annie, and Jack. At least she wasn't fleeing from fire as they had been. Then she remembered Mr Warrender and what might happen and she opened her eyes wide and forced herself forward. It was time to face her fears.

She took the torch and crawled back down into the cold chamber. After moving the matted old cushions with her foot and making sure nothing was hidden underneath, she stood still and looked all around. The only possible hiding place was the bricks, of which there were hundreds. She'd have to systematically go through them all. She thought about George, hiding down here. Clearly he had got away. She hadn't wanted to say the words out loud, but she had been terrified that they might find a tragic pile of bones in the chamber. The relief that George wasn't there made her light headed and determined to put the old, scared Elise behind her. She unwrapped her hands from her sleeves.

She imagined that she was George, running away. It would have been dark, only a chink of light coming in under the door, plus he was short sighted, so he would have had to feel his way around. A loose brick, that's what she needed to find. Mentally she divided the wall into sections, took a deep breath and started the search.

The bricks were cold and slimy and she cringed at the thought of what she was touching. Quickly her nails became dirty and bloodied as she dug her fingers around the bricks. Fear slowed her down as she had to count every brick as she worked. She swallowed back her sobs of fear. Her arms soon began to ache and she was about to stop when a brick suddenly came away in her hand and fell onto the floor, hitting her on the ankle. 'Ouch!' she yelled, her voice reverberating back at her inside the enclosed space.

Her heart began to pound as she lifted the torch and shone it into the hole. Small fat woodlice running around inside the gap made her squeal and step backwards, but the sight of something pale made her squash down her fear. With trembling hands she stuck her fingers into the hole and closed her eyes as she felt around in the dark space. As her finger touched material she pulled her hand back and screamed.

'Elise!' Grace's voice was muffled.

'Stay there, I'm fine,' she yelled back, her voice cracking. She had to prove she could do this. She opened her eyes and pushed her hand back into the space. She carefully squeezed her fingertips around the edges of the material and waited. Nothing happened. She tugged at the cloth. Small stones and bits of dirt flew out with her hand as she pulled the object back out of the gap. She looked down into her palm. What looked like an old handkerchief, folded into a square and tied with string, rested in her hand. With trembling fingers she carefully undid the string and unfolded the cloth, which was damp and stained, but all in one piece. Folded inside was a tiny black book. She swallowed hard, tears prickling at her eyes.

'I think I've found it Annie,' she whispered softly, 'and I've proved something to myself,' she added, before making her way back up into the kitchen. This time she did not need to count the bricks.

'I've found something,' she announced to Grace, who was sitting at the table staring at her phone.

'Really? You mean I don't have to go and scrabble around down in the sewers? Let's see!' She dropped her phone into her bag and pulled her chair closer to the table. Elise placed the handkerchief on the table and then went and rinsed her hands under the tap, before sitting down next to Grace who was studying the cloth from different angles. 'It smells about a hundred years old.'

She told Grace how she had found it as she slowly unwrapped the handkerchief, no longer afraid to touch the material. Holding her breath she opened the book, which was filled with densely written script. Elise read the heading aloud. 'Lightning Lore.' She grabbed Grace's arm. 'We've found it! I can't believe it!'

'Read it to me,' said Grace, 'nice and slowly.'

'It's a whole book!'

'The introduction then.'

Elise cleared her throat, then started reading the words that were written down in front of her. The text was beautifully handwritten, in black ink.

LIGHTNING LORE
I am writing down for you information which has been passed down to

me by my grandfather and his grandfather before him, so that it may forever be preserved amongst our family. The power of lightning has been revealed to the Warrender family but the reasons for this phenomenon are unknown. On the eve of puberty, every male child on the receipt of a stroke of lightning, gains The Gift of mindsight. The lightning strikes in the pupils, enabling the recipient to see into the minds of others, by looking into their eyes. No secret or thought can escape one with The Gift, once they have learned how to master it. Such are the benefits of this gift, that it is every males responsibility to acquire it. In order to facilitate receipt of the power, a special force field has been created, within which the conditions are perfect for acquiring said power. Every father will ensure that his male child is placed within this field on the eve of his thirteenth birthday. As the male child grows, the father will teach the son how to use his Gift, in particular how he may use it to influence the mind of others. It is the responsibility of all males with the Gift to reproduce and ensure that the power is carried down the family line.

Although female members of the family are not encouraged to acquire the Gift, females with the Gift do exist. A Gifted female may exchange thoughts with another who has the Gift, but she is unable to influence the mind of another. However two Gifted females who unite the Circles on their hands are superior in strength, in particular to a single male. Uniting two female hands during a lightning strike may cause harm to those around. By uniting the circular burns on their hands in this way a three way conversation may be had. By this means they are able to influence the will of the male. The male does not have this ability and his power is weakened each time it occurs. A male must never exchange his first mind glance with a girl, as this lessens his power.

Contact with females with The Gift is strongly discouraged.

IT IS IMPERATIVE THAT ALL MALES AVOID BEING STRUCK BY LIGHTNING A SECOND TIME. A SECOND STRIKE REMOVES THE GIFT FROM THE MALE WHO HAS BEEN STRUCK.

Grace whistled. 'So that's what happened when we were on the bus.

The storm must have started. It's amazing that we discovered it by accident.' She raised her hand to Elise for a high five.

'Girl Power!'

Elise stared at the circle, frowning.

'Hey, lighten up Elise, I'm only joking! At least now we know there's a way to stop it.'

'So if Mr Warrender were to be struck by lightning again, he would lose his power. That would stop him terrorizing people.'

'I wonder if he knows about this.'

Grace shrugged.

'It also means that if Jack were to be struck by lightning, he would lose his power?'

Grace nodded. 'So he wouldn't be able to influence other people, in the way that his dad does.'

Elise's eyes were dark. 'I think that's the solution.'

'For Jack to lose his power?'

She wondered how he would feel about that. 'I think it's the only way to free him from his dad.'

A loud banging sound made them both jump. 'It's someone at the front door,' said Elise. 'It might be Jack.' She wrapped the book hastily into the handkerchief. 'Put this in your bag,' she said as she passed it to Grace. The wind had really picked up outside now and the branches of an overhanging tree were banging repeatedly against the window. Elise paled, rubbing her hand instinctively.

'Not another storm, I can't believe it. We need to be really careful, Grace. Mr Warrender...'

'I know.' Grace cut her off. 'Don't say anything about what we've found out to anyone,' she warned.

'Including Jack?'

'Especially Jack.'

Elise went out into the hall, casting a quick glance in the mirror and smoothing down her hair before she opened the door. The wind almost wrenched it out of her hand and she staggered backwards.

'Jack,' she gasped, feeling shy and awkward, her stomach catapulting up and down. He was wearing a dark grey sweatshirt over black jeans, shades and a grey cap. A light dusting of stubble threatened his chin. Rain was coming down hard and she pulled him in quickly, throwing her bodyweight against the door to close it quickly, to keep the storm outside. He reached out and took her hand. His skin was warm.

She pulled her hand away, unsure of him, unsure of everything.

'How's it going?' He stepped back. She couldn't pinpoint what was bothering her.

'Fine.' She shrugged his hand away. 'Come in.'

Seconds after Elise had closed the door, a large shiny car slid silently round the corner past the cottage and stopped alongside the house, out of sight. The driver turned off the engine and looked at his watch. Then he settled down to wait.

CHAPTER 23

'I s Grace here?' Jack was behind her, his voice soft in her ear. She closed the door, drowning out the sound of the heavy rain. She turned, nodding. Something wasn't right.

'Wait,' he said quietly. He took her arm and pulled her into the living room.

'What's up?' she asked. His eyes were bright, and he was fidgeting from one foot to another. 'Grace is in the kitchen. She's waiting for us.'

'I want to speak to you,' he said, 'alone. The thing is, I'm not sure we should trust Grace.'

'You've already said that. What do you mean?'

'She's not been the same since she had that encounter with my dad. He's dangerous. I reckon he may have given her some instructions, got her to betray us in some way.'

'What makes you think that? We were there with her, straight after it happened. She told me everything that he said.'

'How do you know she told you the truth?'

'Because we were mind reading!' Her skin was prickling her and she had to fight off a strong urge to count.

'You can't know that she told you everything,' he persisted..

'A female can't hide stuff, you told us that. It's the men who are good at hiding things, twisting the truth.'

'What are you saying?' His body was still now, his tone cold.

'Nothing,' she stammered, 'women are only powerful when...'

she bit down on her tongue, unsure now.

'When what?' he edged closer. The palm of her hand was itching badly.

'Jack,' she laughed nervously, 'we're talking about Grace here. She's my friend, your friend.'

Elise had a sick feeling in the pit of her stomach. Why was he being like this? She hadn't wanted Grace to be right. She attempted to steer him off the subject. 'How about you? What happened last night? Did you speak to your dad? Were you careful?'

'I didn't speak to him. I stayed in my room until I heard him go out this morning. What about you guys? Did you find anything out?'

Elise relaxed a little as she imagined him sitting in his room alone. Had he been thinking about her? She shook her head slowly. 'I read through some of the documents in the folder, went over the family tree, but nothing jumped out at me. Then Grace came by this morning. She's feeling a lot better.'

'Isn't the weather bothering you?'

She glanced outside as he said this, the rain still battering against the window.

'I've been trying not to think about it.' With a jolt she realised what had been bugging her. Jack had no coat on and his clothes were virtually dry. A shiver ran through her.

'You're cold,' he said, his expression softening. 'Come here.'

'Don't!' she said, too loudly and he stepped back as if she'd struck him. His eyes hardened.

'Why do I get the feeling you're hiding something from me?'

He took a step forward and before Elise could stop him he had ripped her glasses away from her eyes . There was no time to react. They stared at one another. An eerie silence filled the kitchen and Elise became aware of the wind howling outside. She started to shake.

The whooshing sound in her head disappeared almost as soon as it had started. She felt a wave of nausea, then her head cleared and she could see an image of Jack speaking to his father, angry words being said and voices raised. The words were muffled, she couldn't work them out yet.

You did speak to your father! I was right!

Yeah I'm sorry, but I didn't want you to tell Grace. I'm right about her. Dad told me something.

But you know you can't trust him. Everything he says is twisted, that's what you told me before.

He told me that he asked her to help him during the conversation they had. She agreed. He offered her money if she finds what he wants.

I don't believe you! Grace isn't like that!

Exactly how well do you know her?

An image of Grace in her school uniform flew into Elise's mind. Their first meeting, not so long ago.

I can see what you're thinking but you have to believe me.

Jack! I do trust you, but that was before. How do I know you're not trying to manipulate me?'

Why would I do that? You're the one hiding something — what's this black book I can see you're trying so hard not to think about eh?'

Elise's head was pounding but she was unable to stop the thoughts and images from flowing through her mind. She didn't want to but she had no choice. It was too exhausting. As she started to think about the words she'd read a jolt of energy shot through her almost knocking her to the ground. A hand enclosed hers and the burning started up in her palm; she could see Grace's thoughts, mingling with Jack's, pushing his to one side. She was being pulled about and she realised that Jack was trying to free himself from Grace's grip. The circle was like flame in her hand, firing her with energy. After one final effort to pull away Jack slumped, giving in, for it was too late, the circle was in place. Grace relaxed, then concentrated hard, so that her mind went blank, then tuned her attention fully into their conversation.

What have you told him, Elise?

A bit about the Lore, it slipped out, I'm sorry I couldn't help it
.

That's why I had to come in before it was too late ... You're very quiet Jack. There's no point in resisting, two girls are stronger than one boy. The lore says interesting things about us gifted girls. Don't glare at me like that! So what has he been saying about me? Oh I get it, I'm the bad one.

Don't listen to her!

I guess this is where you get to make your mind up Elise. What really happened last night, Jack?

Elise could see the confusion swirling around in Jack's mind, along with something else. Was it guilt? The pressure from Grace's hand intensified. Was she trying to tell her something?

Elise's palm burned as she saw the picture form again, but this time the details were very different. She saw Jack walking past his father's car as he made his way down the drive, his hesitation as he got to the door, then her stomach turned inside out as she saw Jack speaking to his dad, then passing out. Now she could hear Grace's voice, loud in her head.

Is that the kind of person you want to trust Elise? He'd wiped that version from your mind, hadn't he, but we've brought it back. And what's more, we've found something, we've found something that will really help you, enable you to free yourself from your family forever. But we can only share it with you if you make the right decision. Because it's you who has to make the choice now Jack, not Elise. This storm is raging outside and I reckon we're running out of time. So what's it going to be?

Grace held the two hands firmly in hers, both girls watching pictures flying around in Jack's head. Elise could feel his exhaustion pressing down on her own lungs. She couldn't stand his pain, and it was hard for her to breathe.

I want to help you Jack, we both do.

She had to reach out to Jack. She focussed her attention on him. She brought into her mind all the conflicting feelings she had for him.

I can't be friends with you Jack if you lie to me. You tried to manipulate me just now, didn't you? I can see your guilt. Follow your own instincts Jack, you know the right thing to do.

Jack's thoughts went quiet. Then he spoke to her directly.

I'm sorry. You're right. I made up that stuff about Grace. And now you've seen what really happened. But there's something you don't know.

Jack thought about his dad waiting outside in his car. Grace's grip on their hands tightened.

`We have to make a decision now, I'm not going to let go until you've made up your mind and we can see it for ourselves.`

Grace was concentrating so hard that she was totally unprepared for the crash that followed, as the sound of the front door opening let in the howl of the wind, forcing the door to clatter against the wall. Grace jumped, letting go of both hands and the three of them automatically closed their eyes. Elise's head was swimming again, her mum's voice was calling her and she was trying not to lose Jack but he was gone, his mind no longer linked with hers.

'You two stay here,' Grace hissed, pushing past them to get out into the hall. 'I'll see if she's alone.' She glared at Jack, who slumped against the wall and Elise retrieved her shades from the floor and quickly put them on.

'Do you remember what just happened?' she asked, struggling to retrieve her breath. Darkness was closing in on the room and she couldn't stop shivering. Jack's eyes were dark coal against his white face.

'I never thought he'd get to me,' he whispered, so that Elise had to lean in close to catch the words. He looked up at her, his eyes beseeching. 'The last thing I want to do is betray you, you know that, don't you, Elise?' He reached for her hand. She nodded and let her hand relax in his. His skin was cold and she took his fingers between hers, rubbing them briskly to warm them up. Grace had closed the door behind her and the howling wind was making it impossible to hear any voices from outside.

'Wait!' Jack's eyes were wild. 'We have to be careful! Dad's outside. He will bend your mum's mind if he has to, he didn't need to last time but he wanted to make sure she couldn't change her mind.'

'So you've decided to help us.' Elise was so relieved she hardly dared to breathe. She watched his lips as they opened to form a word but the moment was lost as the door slid open and the figure of Mr Warrender loomed in the doorway.

'Jack,' he said, his mouth smiling, his eyes hard like stones. 'I've been so looking forward to this.'

CHAPTER 24

Mum followed Mr Warrender into the room, carrying two bags of shopping.

'Come in Mr Warrender,' she announced. She picked up one of the plastic bags and unloaded four large oranges into the fruit bowl. 'I'll make some tea. Can you light the fire Jack?'

Mr Warrender looked at his watch. 'I haven't got very long actually, I'm meeting with my solicitor at six.'

Mum pulled a face as she piled some bananas on top of the oranges. 'I don't think you should be driving around in this weather,' she said.

Mr Warrender pulled his face into a smile. 'I've lived here all my life. I'm certainly not afraid of a storm. I wouldn't be in this area if I was!'

As if in answer to him, there was a crash outside, as a burst of thunder erupted. Elise jumped.

'There's nothing to be scared of young lady,' Miles said, his eyebrows lifting high up into his forehead. She avoided his eyes, trying to stop herself from scratching her hand, which was itching like crazy. Jack finished piling wood on the fire and sat back down at the table.

'A cup of tea will make you feel better,' Mum said. 'I'll be back in a minute.'

'I'll help you,' Elise said. Jack squeezed her hand under the table, as she stood up. She hoped that meant he was still on their side. The coolness of his skin soothed the circle, which was hot and prickly. She closed the door behind her.

'I like your friends, love,' Mum said as she bustled around arranging cups on a tray. Elise leaned against the worktop, watching her, the heat from under the kettle letting a little warmth into the tiny kitchen.

Mum paused her rattling. 'I can see that Grace is good for you. I spoke to her dad, you know, after the accident. He seems like a really nice man.' Cups arranged, she stopped moving and looked at Elise.

'You've got more colour in your cheeks; I think the country air suits you. Do you miss London?'

Elise cast her mind back to London, picturing herself sitting in her bedroom, dreading the next day at school where it was so difficult to talk to people, teachers who shouted at her when she couldn't answer their questions as she had to finish her counting. She had been counting so much less since that terrible evening.

'No,' she said, 'I like it here. I like the town, it's not so crowded and stressful and people are friendly.' She thought of Sheila, and how helpful she had been, always pleased to see Elise.

'So how would you feel if I sold the cottage?' She leaned over to turn the gas off and poured the water into the teapot. Steam curled up against the cupboard.

'What completely?'

Mum nodded.

Elise tried to imagine not being able to come here. Her insides felt cold. 'I'd hate it,' she said. 'I like it here, Mum. I even wished we lived here.'

'Really?' Mum put the kettle down and looked Elise in the eyes. Elise looked away, blinking furiously. 'Darling, I had no idea.'

Elise bit her lip and swallowed down the tears. 'Things are

getting better for me, Mum. You know what I'm talking about.' She looked away. She never talked about her rituals directly, but Mum knew what was going on. 'And Grace, and Jack,' she hurried on. 'Please don't sell up!' The words burst out of her, straight from the heart, nothing to do with stopping Mr Warrender. She couldn't compete with him, even if she'd wanted to.

'Come here, love.' Mum pulled her in for a hug. Elise buried her face in Mum's cardigan. It felt good, safe. Elise wished she could tell her everything.

'You have nothing to worry about,' Mum said. 'The solicitor advised me not to sell, but I just wanted to double check with you first. I want what's best for you, you know' Now help me with this tray. Mr Warrender said he was in a hurry. I hope he's not going to be too disappointed.'

Elise hugged the news to herself, trying to keep her expression blank as she opened the door, surprised as the wind blew it shut behind them with a loud bang.

'Let's get down to business,' Mr Warrender said as Mum set the tray on the table, sitting down and pulling his briefcase onto his lap, extricating a thin folder. As you know I've come to formalise the offer I made you the other day.'

Mum sighed as she placed a mug down in front of him.

'Actually,' she said, 'I'm going to have to disappoint you, Mr Warrender. Elise and I have made a decision to stay here. I'm not going to sell after all.' Grace looked up at Elise, her face questioning.

Mr Warrender clenched his fists together, his skin turning white. 'I don't understand,' he said. 'Let's go into the sitting room, talk about this privately. I don't really want to do business in front of these kids.'

'No!' Grace was up on her feet. 'Don't go with him!'

'Really, Grace,' Mum said, laughing. 'There's no need to be so dramatic. I don't need to go into the other room, Mr Warrender, as there's nothing more to discuss as far as I'm concerned.'

Mr Warrender was staring at Jack. 'I don't understand. What have you said to her?' he yelled at him, slamming his fist down on the table. 'Why have you let me down?' Elise jumped and Mum also stood up as the vibration of the table made the tea slop out of the mug.

'What are you doing?' she said, staring at Mr Warrender.

'You can't change your mind,' he said, 'look into my eyes and you'll see that you can trust me on this. If it's more money you want …?'

Mum looked horrified. 'No,' she said. 'Please let's be civil about this.'

Mr Warrender turned to Jack, his forehead perspiring. Jack took a step backwards. 'You're behind all this aren't you?'

'Mr Warrender!' Mum started to say as he lunged forwards in an attempt to grab Jack.

'Stop it!' she cried, but her words were lost as the thunder crashed outside, making them all jump.

'Get away from him, Jack!' shouted Grace, as she grabbed Elise's hand, pressing down hard to join the circles. A burst of lightning sliced down from the sky flashing from outside into the room, forcing the back door to burst fully open. Mr Warrender gasped, and for the first time Elise saw his mask crack, fear lighting up his eyes. More thunder followed, Grace and Elise still holding hands, standing now, facing up at the window. The second bolt of lightning sliced into the ground outside the house forcing the glass pane in the window to shatter. Mr Warrender howled as a shard of glass shot into his face and the wind burst through the open door.

'Oh my goodness!' screamed Mum.

'Jack!' shouted Mr Warrender, clutching his face, blood trickling out of a gash in his cheek.

Jack froze, staring at his dad in horror. Grace pulled Elise and they ran over to the back door.

'Help me Jack!' cried Mr Warrender, the menace in his voice absent now, terror in its place. Mum grabbed hold of a tea towel, but he attempted to struggle to his feet.

'Keep still, you're hurt. I'm trying to help you!' She pushed him gently back down. He groaned, collapsing back onto the floor.

Elise looked out into the darkness. Rain was slicing down, splattering all over her feet. A light at the end of the garden flickered. 'Come on Jack,' Grace urged.

Jack's face drained of colour and he looked from Miles to the girls.

'It's time to make your choice Jack,' Grace said.

'But my dad's hurt! He needs me!'

'It's a trick!' Grace shouted, letting go of Elise and pulling Jack towards her. She whirled in front of him and her eyes bored into his.

Are you ready to break your ties with him forever? Free yourself from the Gift?

But my dad is hurt.

Mrs Martin is looking after him. You can't risk looking at him.

What would I have to do?

A second strike of lightning will free you from the Gift, we can take you to the place where Elise got struck, but you need to hurry or it will be too late.

She closed her eyes, releasing him and shouted out 'It's up to you, Jack!'

A rumbling started up in the sky, gathering force until Elise thought her eardrums might burst. Jack grabbed both girls by the hands and they ran to the farthest end of the garden, ending up in the field by the passageway. Rain was pouring down so hard that their clothes were soaked through in an instant. Grace pointed and then Jack was shaking them both free, running as fast as he could, arriving in the centre of the square at the exact moment a silvery yellow burst of lightning shot down out of the sky, slicing through his body. Jack fell to the ground, but the cry of anguish which rose up into the night came from the house, where Mr Warrender was clutching his head, blood now congealing on his cheek.

Elise screamed, throwing herself forward and down onto the floor where Jack lay, his eyes closed, his leg twisted, and wrong. 'Jack!' she gasped, 'are you OK? Speak to me. Look at me.'

Jack slowly opened his eyes. Elise let her breath out. Rain was spiking down over them both, droplets pouring down over her face as she gazed into his eyes searching for answers. His eyes were brown, soft and welcoming, and she waited for the whooshing sound but all she could hear was the wind and the rain. She gulped, wiping the rain away which now was mingling with her tears. She stared harder, just to make sure.

'I can look at you now.' Jack's voice was strained, barely audible above the wind and rain. She took his hand, turning it to look at the palm. The circle was no longer there.

'Grace!' she shouted. 'It worked!'

Suddenly she remembered Mum. 'Mum, where are you?' she called over her shoulder, panic causing her voice to rise. She felt Mum's hands on her shoulders.

'I'm here, darling. I was making sure Mr Warrender was alright.

What on earth has happened? What was the matter with him? Why was he behaving so strangely? I've called an ambulance. Mr Warrender has passed out. Try and stay calm Jack, the paramedics will be here in a minute. I think you may have broken your leg.'

Elise couldn't hold herself together any longer. She fell back against Mum, who wrapped her arms around her tight.

'Let's get you into the warm,' she said.

'No! I'm not leaving Jack. Where's Grace?'

'She went back inside,' Mum said.

Grace appeared at the back door, her silhouette framed in light. She was holding some papers in her hands. She shoved them down inside her jacket. A siren could be heard now, growing louder and louder. Elise closed her eyes as Mum stroked her hair, her body protecting her from the howling wind, and next time she opened them a man in a green outfit was leaning over her, calling her name. Jack was being carried away from her on a stretcher and she reached out and squeezed his hand as he went past. Mr Warrender was next, a breathing mask on his face as he was loaded into the ambulance, Mum following them. She let out a sigh of relief.

'I heard that,' Grace said, as she knelt down at her side.

'Why did you go back in there?' asked Elise.

Grace pulled the papers out from under her jacket. 'Just in case,' she said. 'I wouldn't trust him not to forge a signature, even if he was lying on the floor.' She held the papers out in front of her, large drops of rain plopping down and sliding across the paper. The water turned Mr Warrender's signature inky blue, disappearing in seconds.

'We've done it!' Elise whispered, the enormity of what Jack had done only hitting her then. 'Jack's lost the Gift.' Her teeth started chattering as the rain cascaded down on her head. She almost didn't believe it was true.

Grace lifted several wet strands of hair out of Elise's eyes. The paramedic was approaching them again and Grace helped him escort Elise to the ambulance.

'You're in shock,' he explained. 'I'm taking you both to hospital. Your mother's coming with you.'

They waited for Mum in the ambulance as she was speaking to the paramedic outside. She clambered in and squeezed into a seat on the side. The first ambulance revved it's engine, then set off down the road, siren blaring.

'Why have they put the siren on Mum? It's not Jack is it? Elise's heart started to batter against her chest, drowning out the sound of the rain on the roof.

Mum shook her head. 'Jack is fine,' she said, but her expression was dark. 'But his father isn't. They suspect Mr Warrender has had a heart attack.'

CHAPTER 25

Grace was standing outside the library, talking into her phone.

'Who was that?' Elise asked as she finished the call and slid the phone back into her pocket.

Grace grinned. 'Will. He's come to his senses and dumped that stupid girl. He's begging me to go back with him now.'

'And will you?'

Grace pouted. 'I'll make him sweat for a while, let him be extra nice to me for a bit. Then I'll see. But forget that,' she said, slipping her arm through Elise's, leading her away from the library. 'What about you and Jack?'

'It's going well. We're going for a picnic this afternoon. It's so different now I don't have to worry about the mind reading. I was scared to even think when I was with him before!'

Elise and Grace hadn't gone to Mr Warrender's funeral. This afternoon would be the first time she had seen him since.

'What's the address again?'

'24 Castle Avenue. It's the next street on the left I think.'

Elise had sent Sheila a message to tell her about the happenings at the cottage. Sheila had phoned back that same evening. As soon as her grandmother Elizabeth had heard what had happened, she'd insisted on seeing Elise.

'It's really strange,' Sheila had said. 'From refusing to even think about the past she seems desperate now to talk about it.'

Sheila opened the door to them and gave both girls a big hug. They followed her into a beautiful sitting room, where a tiny little bird of a woman sat on a green velvet couch, a blanket covering her knees. Her eyes were shiny as they flittered about over the girls' faces.

'Hello,' she said, her voice light and fragile. 'I'm Elizabeth. Which of you is Elise?'

Elise lifted her hand. Elizabeth's eyes rested on her for a moment, before turning to look at Grace. 'So you must be Grace. Sit down dears, but you might need to pull your chairs up closer. I can't see very well these days. I'd like some tea a little later please Sheila, but first I'd like to speak to the girls. You don't mind leaving us alone for a bit do you, dear?'

The girls pulled the two armchairs closer to Elizabeth as Sheila left the room.

'I've never told anyone this before,' she said, 'because my mother swore me to secrecy at the time and I was always afraid of the Warrenders. But now that Mr Warrender is dead I know that it is the right thing to do. And I want to tell it before my time is up here, because I know it is approaching now.'

'No,' Grace said, 'you don't know that. Lots of people live to be a hundred these days. The Queen spends all her time sending telegrams.'

'I don't think she'll be sending me one dear.' Grace locked eyes with Elise.

She knows

Yes

Elizabeth coughed and they unlocked eyes.

'I'm almost blind,' she said, 'so come closer to me so I can feel you near me. Give me your hands.'

Elise felt her stomach turnover as she caught sight of the faint blue circle on Elizabeth's papery hand and realised what was happening. Elizabeth took one of each of their hands in her own, a slight tremor evident before the warmth started, as their hands enclosed and their minds were linked.

My voice gets tired now I am so old, so this makes it easier for me. Yes I have the Gift, like my grandmother before me. She told me about the Gift she had when I was a little girl, and about the field behind the house where she was struck. Curiosity got the better of me, and one day when she was out and a storm was raging I went out into the field. I didn't believe it would work, but how wrong I was!

I knew the two of you were gifted as soon as you set foot in the room. My Gift has changed as I get older and my eyesight fails me. It's lovely to feel your soft warm hands, your skin so young. Sheila knows nothing of this, this story is for the gifted alone. And yes Elise, I hear your question. You can tell Jack. But there is someone else far more important who needs to know.

Annie?

Yes, Annie. My grandmother beseeched me to use my Gift to find Annie, and I have waited all my life not daring to depart without releasing her. I knew she was trapped but had no way of finding her. Once I have told you what happened to George I will be able to rest in peace.

This is my grandmother's story. She went to find George on that terrible day after Annie had fled the house. She had to know what caused her such distress and made her fly out of the house like that. She went to find him and imagine her horror at seeing the state of his face. He was frantic to leave but she would not let him go until he told her what was happening.

She waited and waited for him to return, then when she saw Mr Warrender leave the house she followed him for she could stand it no longer and a huge fear was eating her up inside. As she ran towards the cottage she saw an orange glow in the sky and she knew then that the cottage was on fire. My grandmother was on fire too as she ran so fast, stumbling and sobbing but by the time she reached the cottage it was too late. She tried to get in but some men had gathered and they stopped her from entering, even though she screamed that people were inside.

She was desolate that evening, Grandmother had to give her something to calm her down, and she thought she was hallucinating later that night when she heard a knocking at her window and George's face appeared. He was black and sooty but he was the sweetest vision she ever saw. He explained that he had escaped via the passage and that he was leaving and never coming back. He swore her to secrecy but promised that he would keep in touch.

My mother received a letter from him exactly one year later, telling her that he could no longer live with the burden of the Gift and the curse of his family, and that by the time she received this letter he would have departed this world. She went immediately to the address on the letter but it was too late. The poor child had rid himself of the burden of being a son of Warrender, but he was unaware that his mother had brought another child into the world, unfortunately a son, thus the family evil was able to continue. Mother feared that George took his life in vain, but he did not want to live without Annie. If you can tell her what happened to him, then she will be able to rest in peace.

Elizabeth closed her eyes and slowly let her hands drop away from theirs. She opened her eyes, blinking at the sudden daylight.

'So George was also trapped, wondering where Annie was,' Grace said. 'Do you think they can be reunited now?'

'I rather think that's up to Elise, don't you?' Elizabeth smiled. 'I'm glad that you girls have kept your Gift. It's a good thing in the end. Otherwise you would never have been able to help Annie.'

Elise nodded. 'I know what I have to do, I'm just waiting for the weather to change.'

'Funny that,' said Elizabeth, 'I knew the build up of storm recently wasn't normal. I sensed something was happening, and was terrified as to what it could be. When Sheila came home and told me a young girl was asking questions about the Warrenders, well, let's just say I've had many sleepless nights since then and I've prayed for you every night.'

'There is one more thing,' Elise said. 'The Lightning Lore.'

Elizabeth's eyes too on a faraway look. 'A Lightning Lore, you've taken me right back there. I've heard talk of that, but I can't tell you anything about it, I'm afraid. In fact, to be honest I never really believed in its existence.'

Elise exchanged a surprised look with Grace.

'We've found it, Elizabeth, Grace and I, we searched the passage beneath the house. I suppose you couldn't possibly have known.'

'How did you know where to look?'

'I pieced information together, what Annie told me, Mary's diary. We realised that had to be what Mr Warrender was looking for and once we found about the passage from the diary – Mary actually mentions the fact that Arthur is building a passage under the house.'

Elizabeth's eyes were shining now. 'I don't suppose you have it on you?'

Elise shook her head.

'We can probably remember a lot of it,' Grace said. 'The main message it gives is that women are more powerful when they have the Gift, which is how it should be, of course.'

Elizabeth chuckled. 'I'd love to see it.'

'Of course, I'll bring it over to show you,' Elise said. 'But that's what I was going to say anyway, before I realised you didn't know that we'd found it. I'm giving it to you, and you can decide what to do with it.'

'That's very kind of you, child. I'm so looking forward to seeing it. But now that Mr Warrender has gone, my decision is easy. On my death I will donate it to the museum, that will make Sheila happy.'

There was a tapping sound at the door.

'Is it safe to come in?' The door opened and Sheila stood in the doorway holding a tray. Old fashioned cups and saucers delicately painted in blue and white detail rattled as she crossed the room. Grace eyed the three tiered stand full of cakes and winked at Elise. Sheila poured the tea, handed out the cups and then sat down on the sofa.

'Well I hope you've all had an interesting chat,' she said, stirring sugar into her cup. 'Gran has already told me all about it.' A little smile flickered around Elizabeth's lips, causing her face to crinkle. Elise bit down on her lip to stop herself from laughing, and Grace busied herself with her cup.

As they left the house Sheila drew Elise into a hug.

'Thank you,' Elise said. 'For everything.'

Sheila looked questioningly at her.

'For helping me settle in around here. You know we're moving to Eldon permanently? I'm starting at St Saviours's in September.'

Grace rolled her eyes. 'You won't be so pleased when you're stuck in double maths with Mr Conway. Come on, Elise, you've got a hot date to get ready for.'

CHAPTER 26

The sun was high in the sky, a cool breeze lifting the sand as it blew, scattering it all over the picnic blanket.

'I can't believe it's actually getting warm,' Elise said, 'no more horrible storms.'

'Well don't get too excited, rain is forecast later in the week.'

Elise groaned. 'Let's make the most of it then. Are you hungry?' She looked over at Jack, still not used to the novelty of being able to look him in the eyes. A slow smile lit across his face. Now that Jack no longer had the Gift, they couldn't stop looking at each other. After they'd eaten the last crumb of baguette and shared the last drop of old fashioned lemonade, they lay down on the soft tartan blanket and looked up at the sky together.

'Is your Mum OK?' asked Elise, tracing the wisps of clouds with her eyes, the breeze fluttering through her hair.

Jack pushed himself up onto his elbow, so that he could see Elise's face.

'I think she's relieved. It was a massive shock of course, but now she's free. She's selling the house, moving somewhere smaller. Has Sarah decided what she's doing about the cottage yet?

Elise nodded, now it was her turn to sparkle. 'Mum's finally made up her mind! We're moving into a flat in Eldon while she fixes up the cottage. I'm going to enrol at St Saviours in September. We'll live in the cottage eventually.' She looked into Jack's eyes, marvelling at the warm hazel colour, now so familiar to her.

'Do you miss it at all – the Gift, I mean? It must be weird, not having it any more.'

'No,' he said. 'It was like a curse. I know you still have yours, but you can only mind read with others who have it. At times I was scared to go out of the house, for fear of accidentally tripping into someone's mind. I felt like a criminal! I mean who wants to know what their mother is really thinking? And as for you, well, I was terrified that you might not like me!'

'I'm glad we didn't tell Mum in the end.' Elise knew Mum wouldn't have believed a word of it. She'd overheard her discussing 'Mr Warrender's mental health problems' with Grace's dad, who'd been popping round to see Mum rather a lot lately.

'I don't understand why Dad hadn't bent her mind. After the meeting they had, and she was so ready to sell up to him, I assumed that's what had happened.'

'He didn't need to. Mum was tempted by his offer, but as soon as she realised I was happy here, it was too late. She could see how much better I was down here.' Elise had told Jack all about her rituals. Somehow, now that she had the choice of what to tell him, she found that she wanted him to know all about her. Just as she wanted to find out everything there was to know about him.

'It's lucky he never got hold of the Lightning Lore, otherwise who knows what he might have done.' Jack rolled onto his back, taking her hand in his and all she could hear was the lapping of the sea in the distance.

She laughed out loud.

'What?' asked Jack.

'I was wondering what you were thinking – you don't know how good that feels.'

'Do you really want to know what was in my head at that very precise moment?'

She nodded, her eyes lighting up.

He stroked her fringe away from her eyes. 'I was wondering whether you would mind if I kissed you just there,' he touched her neck, 'right on that very cute mole.'

'What do you think?' she smiled.

His lips brushed her neck softly. She put her arms around his waist and they lay quietly, little puffs of his soft breath dusting over her skin.

Elise sighed. 'I don't want this weather to end, ever, but without a storm I can't speak to Annie. I'm scared I'll never get to speak to her again. Maybe she lost her power too. What if she never gets to hear the answers to her question? I couldn't bear it.'

'I'm sure she hasn't lost her power. You and Grace can still communicate can't you?' She nodded.

A silence rested between them for a moment, the breeze rustling through the trees the only audible sound.

'How was the funeral?' she asked 'Was it hard?'

Jack lay back down again, reaching for her hand with his own.

'Horrible, sad, a relief. So many different things. Mum held it together most of the way through until we got back to the house actually. Then she just sort of collapsed. There was a really old lady there, someone said she was almost a hundred. There was something about her, she had a kind of aura about her, like I felt around your painting. I meant to ask Mum who she was.'

'I think I know,' said Elise, propping herself up on one elbow to look down at Jack. She told him what had happened yesterday, after the visit to the library. 'I'm giving Elizabeth the Lightning Lore. She's going to donate it to the museum. She couldn't believe we'd found it, in fact she didn't believe it really existed. She's dying you know, but she's happy.' She looked down at the faint scar on his hand, the circle only faintly visible now. 'And I'm happy too in a funny sort of way.'

So when the storm broke that evening, Elise had told Mum not to let anyone disturb her and here she was, locked in her room with the photograph. For the last time she looked into Annie's world, finally able to tell her what she had waited so long to discover. She settled herself down beside the window, exhaled loudly, and smoothed the photograph out onto her lap. She'd waited ages for this storm, it was as if the last had been so momentous it had wiped all other storms out of existence, the rain fading away as Mr Warrender took his last breath. But this morning, when she had opened her eyes to a darkening room, she'd watched as bulging clouds had drifted across the sky, one by one until the light was blocked out. Now, as the lightning crackled in the sky, safely outside and away from her, she took a deep breath and stared down into Annie's eyes.

Annie's eyelashes fluttered open, and her eyes filled with hope.

Elise! You've been gone so long, I thought you weren't coming back. I was afraid you'd failed.

I've been busy

I can see something different in your eyes

There's so much to tell you

Did you find out about George?

Yes

You look sad

Are you sure you want me to tell you?

I have to know George's fate, whatever it was.

So Elise told Annie the story, everything that had happened. Once shee had finished speaking both girls were silent. Tears filled Elise's eyes and spilled over onto the photograph.

Thank you Elise. I can finally rest.

Annie's eyes shimmered around the edges and slowly began to lose their focus. Elise stared as hard as she could, but was unable to keep the image in her mind. As the photograph blurred in front of her, she knew that Annie was gone forever. She let the tears fall until they were done, then she placed the photograph on the shelf next to her bed.

ACKNOWLEDGEMENTS

I would like to thank all those people who supported me throughout the writing process, especially The Next Chapter girls - Cler, Becky and Louise, the BackachYA girls - Sophie, Debbie, Christina, Morag and Mel, Sheepa, Julakha, Nariece and Elise for reading earlier versions and of course Paul for putting up with my general madness!

ABOUT THE AUTHOR

www.lesleycheetham.com

Lesley Cheetham is a Secondary School librarian in London. She studied French and Theatre Studies at Warwick University. She lives in Kings Cross with her husband. When she isn't writing in coffee bars she enjoys reading, writing, swimming, running and languages. Lesley's debut novel, *Her Sister's Voice*, won the Islington Teen Read Award, 2014.